BELIEVING LOVE

WELCOME TO HARDY FALLS

BETSY HORVATH

VARIOUS MINDED BOOKS

Various Minded Books
PO Box 792
Quakertown, PA 18951
Email: admin@variousmindedbooks.com
www.variousmindedbooks.com

Publisher's Note: This is a work of fiction. Names, characters, places, and incidents are a product of the author's imagination. Locales and public names are sometimes used for atmospheric purposes. Any resemblance to actual people, living or dead, or to businesses, companies, events, institutions, or locales is entirely coincidental.

Edited by: Kendra L. Clayton

Believing Love / Betsy Horvath. -- 1st ed.
ISBN 978-1-943725-04-5

This one's for you, Mom, with lots and lots of love. Thanks for everything.

ACKNOWLEDGMENTS

Many thanks to all of the wonderful people who have believed in me through the years. I'm sure I didn't make it easy for them! And I'm grateful most of them still talk to me.

Special thanks to my wonderful, hard-working, editor, Kendra Clayton. I tried to be good and do what she told me to do, but, well, sometimes I rebelled. I take full responsibility for any inappropriate grammar, comma usage, or sentence structure. Typos are the computer's fault.

And–last but definitely not least–huge, big, heaping helpings of thanks to everyone who reads this book!

1

June Esperanza was crouching behind the old wooden bar that dominated the empty taproom of the Country Time Bar and Grill putting away some napkins when she heard the tavern's front door open and quick, light, footsteps echoing across the antique planked floor.

What the hell? They were closed for another hour, and the door should have been locked. Hannah must have forgotten to secure it again when she'd gone to get some stuff for the party they were hosting later that evening.

June stood, ready to throw out the intruder, but hesitated when she saw an elderly woman standing in the middle of the room looking around with a vague expression. Her white hair was cut in a short, stylish bob, and she was clutching a large purse to her thin chest. She looked familiar, although June couldn't quite place her. She just knew she didn't belong there.

"I'm sorry, ma'am," she said, leaning her forearms on top of the bar. "We're not open."

The woman turned, chocolate brown eyes wide and confused in an oval face, and June drew in her breath.

Eva Hardy in the flesh, by God. Unofficial queen of Hardy

Falls, the little, pissant, whitewashed, Pocono Mountain tourist-trap town where the Country Time was located, and where June had, for some inexplicable reason, lived for the last sixteen years or so.

"Mrs. Hardy," she said, straightening away from the bar. "What are you doing here?" Her voice was cold, but she couldn't help that. She hadn't spoken to Eva in years—hadn't even seen the woman in at least three—and could happily have gone a while longer without renewing their acquaintance.

Instead of giving her the confident, superior, smile June remembered so well, Eva appeared even more confused, her dark brows furrowed over her thin nose.

"Do I know you?"

"Yes," June said slowly, belatedly remembering that Eva had early-onset Alzheimer's disease. It had apparently gotten significantly worse over the past year, which was why Calvin had moved back to town three months ago.

Calvin Hardy. The only child of Ronald and Eva Hardy.

And an asshole.

"No, I don't. I don't know you." Eva threw back her shoulders, the habitual movement emphasizing how thin she was now. "Where's Fred? I'm looking for Fred," she demanded querulously.

Fred? Was she talking about Fred Frederickson, Hannah's father? Yeah, he used to own the Country Time, but he'd been dead for more than two years. Hannah ran things now.

"Ah, he's not here," June said, trying to think of what to do. She moved cautiously out from behind the bar and walked toward the other woman, not wanting to say or do anything to upset her more. Did people with Alzheimer's get violent? June didn't think so, but she didn't want to find out. All she'd need would be for Chief Kline to arrest her for getting into a smackdown with Ronald Hardy's fragile, little wife.

But how the hell was she going to get her out of there?

Christ, was Eva still driving? If she'd driven, June would feel obligated to make sure she got home, which would be the freaking cherry on top of her freaking day.

Eva frowned. "But Fred told me to come. We made arrangements to meet here."

Interesting. June hadn't known Eva and Fred were that close.

She considered the other woman for a moment. Even with the ravages of her disease imprinted on her face, she was still lovely and had probably been quite a babe when she was younger. For his part, Fred had been one hell of a good-looking man. Heck, June had actually given some thought to the highly inappropriate proposition he'd made to her when she'd first started working for him, even though he'd been a good twenty-five years her senior.

In the end, she'd decided against it. He hadn't been married —Hannah's mother had been killed in a car crash a few years before June blew into town—but there had still been too many complications to make it worthwhile.

Fred sure hadn't liked it when she'd turned him down, though. Over the years, she'd discovered that most women came running when Fred showed interest.

Had Eva been one of them? She'd certainly been a Country Time regular back in the day, spending many an evening here at the bar talking to Fred after bowling with the leagues next door at Murphy Lanes. If June remembered correctly, Eva's husband had rarely joined in the discussions.

"I'm sorry," she said, taking another step toward the woman. Eva pulled her handbag closer to her chest, as if afraid June would steal it.

Yeah, because that's just what I would do, huh?

Stop it, June ordered herself. *She doesn't mean anything. She's old and scared and confused and doesn't even realize she knows you.*

"Fred isn't here now," she said, trying to be kind. She was

usually better at slapping sense into a person, but she could be kind if she felt like it. Hannah would attest to that. "Do you want to sit down and wait for him? Maybe have some coffee?" If she stalled until Hannah got back, she could dump the whole situation on her. After all, she was the one who'd forgotten to lock the door.

Still clutching her purse like a security blanket, Eva glanced around the room, at the small wooden tables gleaming with polish, the stained glass lanterns hanging above them, and the flat-screen television over the bar.

"It's...nice in here," she said hesitantly, putting a hand to her forehead.

"Sit down," June said, and this time the kindness was natural. "Come on. I'll get you some coffee, and we'll talk."

"Okay." Eva sounded heartbreakingly young. She tried to pull out one of the sturdy wooden chairs at a nearby table, and June hastened forward to help when it looked like the effort might cause her to topple over.

Once seated, the older woman looked up and smiled a beautiful smile, clean and clear and bright. June blinked. Eva Hardy had never smiled at her like that before.

"You're very nice," Eva said. "Do I know you?"

June drew in a deep breath. "No," she said. "We've never met." Because she had never met this version of the woman.

"Oh." Eva beamed. "I hope we'll be friends."

June didn't know what to say to that, so she turned and went behind the bar where a massive coffee machine sat on the back counter, a full pot simmering on its burner. She got a clean mug, poured coffee, then doctored it with a couple packs of sugar and the last of the half-and-half from the open carton in the refrigerator under the bar. *Sweet and light.*

Moving with the ease of long practice, she took the mug of coffee to the other woman and put it down in front of her. Eva smiled that young smile again, then lifted it with both hands and sipped.

"It's perfect," she said, putting the mug carefully back down on the table. "You knew just how I like it."

The comment made June pause. How had she remembered that? She'd served an awful lot of coffee to an awful lot of people in the years since she'd last seen Eva.

She guessed some things just stayed with you, whether you wanted them to or not.

As if on cue, the front door slammed open, and a man came rushing in.

"Mom? Mom, are you...?" his voice trailed off, and he skidded to a halt.

Calvin. The bastard.

June had tried to prepare herself for the impact of seeing him again after fifteen years, but the reality still punched her in the gut. She stared at him—at the thick, dark hair, now liberally sprinkled with silver, the dark eyes, so like his mother's, glittering in his hard face, the broad shoulders, and the long, muscled legs.

"June," he said, his voice deep and soft, a velvet growl.

June forced herself to remain casual, arms crossed, chin up.

"Calvin."

He swallowed.

"I—"

"Do I know you?" Eva asked primly from her seat at the table.

Calvin shook himself and switched his focus to his mother, allowing June to take her first deep breath since he'd burst into the room.

"Mom," he said. "I've been looking all over for you."

"I'm sorry," Eva said, folding her hands in her lap. "I don't believe we've met."

The expression on Calvin's face was easy to define—it was grief. He glanced at June quickly, as if embarrassed.

"She's been pretty bad today," he said apologetically. "Usually she recognizes my father and me."

A twinge of sympathy had June speaking more gently than she'd intended.

"She says she's looking for Fred," she told him.

"We're meeting here," Eva chimed in, smiling.

"I told her he wasn't in," June finished.

Eva frowned at her. "Did you? Do I know you?"

"Um, okay." Calvin was obviously confused, but he knelt down next to his mother, his large hand on the wooden arm of the chair. "Fred called the house, um, ma'am. He can't see you today."

"Oh." Eva's smooth face creased with dismay. "Really?"

"Yes. Why don't you come with me? I'll make sure you get back home."

"No. I don't know you." Eva looked at June. "Should I trust him?"

Not on your life. "I'm sure you can."

As if that settled the matter, Eva nodded, then finished her coffee. "How much do I owe you?" she asked June.

"On the house."

Eva let Calvin help her to her feet. "I want to go home," she told him.

"That's where we're going." Calvin looked back over his shoulder at June as he led his mother from the room. "Thank you," he mouthed.

June nodded.

Then they were gone, and she was alone again.

Calvin Hardy.

"Shit." June sank down on the chair Eva had just vacated.

She'd known she'd see him some time, she reminded herself. She'd heard he'd rejoined his old bowling league—

God only knew why—and since most of the bowlers came to the Country Time to eat and drink after their scheduled matches, he was bound to show up sooner or later. It was actually kind of a miracle it had taken three months for them to run into each other.

June exhaled.

At least their first encounter was over now. She'd seen him again. They'd spoken. She'd survived. So, it would be easier next time.

Right?

Pushing herself to her feet, she went to the front door, locked it, then turned to look at the taproom. It glowed gold in the lamplight, with scattered patches of color decorating the tables and floor from the early afternoon sun shining through the old stained glass windows.

Back when she'd been twenty-two, the Country Time had seemed like just another dump. She'd never expected to stay longer than it took to save up enough money to hit the road again. No one had been more surprised than she when it had become home. No one had been more shocked that she'd stayed on in spite of everything.

Sighing, she walked back to the bar and continued with the preparations for opening. She wished to hell she hadn't come in early to help Hannah get ready for the party they were hosting that night. If she hadn't been working, she wouldn't have seen Calvin again. She wouldn't have seen Eva. And she wouldn't have seen how delicate and frail the woman was, seen the hurt in Calvin's dark eyes when she didn't recognize him.

What must that be like—to have your own mother not recognize you?

June snorted. She got a clean rag from the stack under the bar and began polishing the wooden top until it shone, rubbing hard to erase any marks or bottle rings.

Hell, in her case it would've been a miracle if her mother

had known who she was in the first place. By the time June had turned three, all Leila Esperanza had cared about had been her next fix. If June's grandmother hadn't stepped in, she didn't know where she'd have ended up. Child Protective Services, probably.

Too bad Grandma Rose had decided to correct the mistakes she'd made with Leila by regimenting every moment of her granddaughter's life. June had been bound to rebel, hadn't she? Guys and bikes, cigarettes and drinking. No drugs, though. She'd seen what it had done to her mother. Leila had been a walking skeleton, her whole life plunged into her veins along with the heroin. She'd died when June had been eight, but it had hardly mattered.

It *had* mattered when Grandma Rose died of a heart attack, but June had been seventeen and not about to go into foster care, thank you very much. Instead, she'd dumped school and hit the road.

Five years and a lot of miles later, she'd ended up in Hardy Falls with Fred and Hannah.

And Calvin.

2
___

Fortunately, before June could wander any further down memory lane the kitchen door opened, and Hannah Frederickson sidled into the room.

June blinked in surprise.

"Care to tell me why you're carrying a fake palm tree?" she asked.

Hannah grinned at her through the mass of plastic leaves. "It's for Bob's party," she said, sliding behind the bar and walking past June to put the phony plant in a corner. She adjusted the branches, then stepped back and studied the result with evident satisfaction. "Perfect. I've got nine more in the car. We can put them everywhere. Isn't it awesome?"

June considered the tree. It was over four feet tall and such a toxic shade of green that she expected it to send out poisonous gas.

"Awesome," she agreed.

Hannah rubbed her hands together. "I got a lot of other great stuff at the dollar store, too. Wait until you see."

"Great." June felt some trepidation, but Hannah was so

pleased with herself she couldn't help but smile along with her. She maybe even felt a bit of a maternal affection for the girl.

Okay, not maternal. She wasn't *that* much older. But big-sisterly. Or auntly. Hannah might be her boss now, but to June she'd always be the gangly, wide-eyed, thirteen-year-old kid she'd met sixteen years ago.

Hannah looked over at her, expression turning serious. "Thanks for coming in early to help with the prep, by the way. Deacon would have done it, but this is supposed to be his day off. It's bad enough he's coming in to work at the party."

"No problem. Not like I had a lot else to do."

Since it was summer, she had originally planned on using the afternoon to take some photographs of the gardens Mathilda Gregory, her landlady and the town's librarian, nurtured throughout the year. June loved the way the flowers and shrubs tumbled around Ms. Gregory's white house, loved being able to look out the windows of her tiny apartment perched on top of the garage and see all of the colors spread out below.

She had decided to frame a montage of the landscape through the seasons and give it to the other woman as a Christmas present, so she wanted to take some pictures in the summer. But there was no real rush, and Hannah had needed her.

June threw the used rag into a laundry tub, then got a new one and took it and the spray bottle of cleaning fluid to wipe down the tables.

As she worked, she hid a smile, because it was so pathetically obvious Hannah had a thing for Deacon Black, her hottie of a bartender, and was totally oblivious to the fact. She was certain Deacon had a thing for Hannah. The two had known each other in high school, but Hannah had hooked up with Deacon's brother Sam—twice. Sam, the asshole, had broken her heart—twice.

Now that Deacon was finally back in town after serving in the army and then drifting around the country, June hoped Hannah would get her head out of her butt, realize she'd picked the wrong Black brother, and give the right one a chance.

Noticing the empty coffee mug Eva had used, she picked it up and took it to the bus tub under the bar.

"Was someone else here?" Hannah asked absently. She was struggling to open a new carton of half-and-half without much success. "Damn it! Why do they always make these things so hard to open? Why can't we get milk with those plastic pouring thingies, instead?" She picked at the gable top of the carton with a fingernail, trying to pull up the spout.

"Just give me the freaking thing." June took the container away from her and opened it easily.

"I hate you." Hannah snatched the milk back and doctored the coffee she'd poured for herself. She sipped, then sighed reverently before looking at June again. "So, who was here?"

"What makes you think anyone was here?" June hedged, going back to the tables.

"Because that's not your mug, and you're avoiding the question." Hannah frowned, her own coffee mug cradled between her palms. "Did Pat show up again? I told you that if he starts stalking you—"

"No, it wasn't Pat."

Pat Murphy, owner of Murphy Lanes, the bowling alley next door to the Country Time, just couldn't seem to accept the fact that he and June were through, even though June had told him often enough that she didn't want to date him anymore. He'd taken to dropping in at odd hours, which was getting really awkward. But it was her own damned fault. She was the one who'd made the huge mistake of hooking up with him again one night after she'd heard Calvin was moving back to town.

June grabbed the bottle of cleaning fluid and sprayed the

nearest table top, then bent over it and polished with more force than was necessary. She realized she didn't want to tell Hannah what had happened, which was stupid. It wasn't like it was that big of a deal.

"You forgot to lock the door," she said, moving to the next table. "Eva Hardy wandered in."

"Oh. How is she?" Hannah asked. "I hear the Alzheimer's has gotten pretty bad."

"Bad enough." June remembered the look of hurt on Calvin's face. "She sure didn't seem to know what was going on." And she certainly hadn't remembered June, or she would never have flashed that bright, innocent smile.

Hannah shook her head. "Poor thing."

"Yeah." Although June had never in a million years thought she'd consider the regal Eva to be "poor." "She was looking for your father."

"Really?" Hannah put her mug down on the bar, then leaned on the top next to it, hands clasped. "That's weird. She hasn't set foot in the Country Time for years."

"No," June agreed without inflection.

Hannah was watching her carefully. "Okay, so Mrs. Hardy's not here now. What happened? Did someone come to get her?"

"Yes." June turned to the next table and sprayed the cleaning fluid. "Calvin came."

Hannah was silent until June met her eyes again.

"That must have been hard," the younger woman said quietly. "I'm sorry."

See? This was the problem with staying in one place for a long time. People knew all kinds of shit about you.

"It was okay," June said, and she almost believed it. "I had to see him again sometime. It's only amazing we didn't run into each other before now." Man, that was becoming her freaking mantra.

"Right." Hannah's voice was thick with sympathy.

"Look," June threw down her rag and faced Hannah more fully, planting her hands on her hips. "Calvin and me—that was a long time ago, and it's over. He moved on. I moved on. End of story. Am I thrilled he's come back to town? No. But I can deal with it."

Hannah studied her, her hazel eyes as solemn as they'd been when she was a kid.

"Of course you can," she said.

June shifted.

"We'd better get busy if you want to get this dump decorated before we open," she said, desperate to change the subject. "When is everyone else supposed to show up?"

Hannah was silent for another moment, then apparently decided to let it drop. She glanced at the clock.

"They should be here any minute now. I wanted to have a meeting before we opened to make sure everyone was ready for the party. We're going to be insanely busy tonight."

June was sure she was right. Bob Johnson, the only attorney in town, was retiring. The story was that the big, beefy, silver-haired lawyer was leaving his practice to become a missionary in Indonesia, which was why Hannah had decided to turn a local bar into an island paradise.

Personally, June thought it was the biggest load of horse shit she'd ever heard. Bob Johnson as a missionary was so laughable she couldn't imagine why anyone even pretended to believe it.

On the other hand, the party was sure to bring a ton of business to the Country Time. Bob had invited everyone he knew, and since he pretty much knew the whole town she expected the joint would be jumping. Tips should be awesome. She'd put up with poisonous plastic plants and grabby-hands Bob for that.

Before she could comment, the kitchen door opened, and Deacon Black strode into the room, grinning.

"Hey, you're—" Hannah broke off abruptly when she got a good look at him. "What the hell are you wearing?" she demanded.

Deacon's grin widened, and he spread his impressive arms, doing a runway turn to show off his bright tangerine-colored Hawaiian shirt, decorated with fluorescent pink flamingos kicking up long pink legs.

"Like it?" he asked.

"Wow." Hannah shook her head in wonder. "I said everyone should wear something tropical, not nuclear."

"That is the ugliest shirt I've ever seen," June told him honestly.

Deacon chortled and dropped his hands. "Just what I was aiming for," he said. "Let's get this show on the road."

A short time later, the tables were wiped down, the place was mostly decorated, and the rest of the staff had arrived. Once all hands were on deck, so to speak, June slipped off to the restroom and changed into a stiff cotton shirt she'd purchased specifically for the occasion. It was a thrift store find and ugly as sin—bright green fabric covered with large-ass gold and silver leaves. True, they were oak leaves, not palm fronds, but she figured once the party got going nobody would care anyway.

After stuffing the old T-shirt she'd been wearing into her purse, she returned to the taproom and settled on a bar stool, leaning back with her elbows on the wooden top of the bar behind her. It was nice to sit down for a few minutes.

The place actually looked pretty good. Hannah's virulent, green plastic palm trees were scattered here and there, adding a kitschy charm. She'd also picked up some pineapples at the grocery store, and they were set out on the tables as center-pieces. June hoped they wouldn't turn into fruit missiles once the drinks were flowing freely. She'd have to keep an eye on Old Albert Cromwell and his cronies, in case they got feisty.

The scrape of a chair being pulled across the floor grabbed her attention, and she turned her head to see Mary Alice Norton, one of the other servers, festive in a particularly alarming scarlet blouse covered with bird of paradise blossoms. She was climbing up on the seat to hang more streamers from a banner that said "Good Luck, Bob." June pushed away from the bar.

"Mary Alice, I don't think—"

The other woman wobbled precariously, and Hannah hustled over to give her a hand.

Relieved, June settled again. In her opinion, Mary Alice should just give it a rest. She'd already hung enough blue and green streamers to choke a horse. Bob wasn't going to give a damn anyway. Rum was about the only tropical thing he cared about.

There was a rustle of movement, and Deacon, on the other side of the bar, leaned across the top near her.

"That was close," he said. "Mary Alice shouldn't climb on top of things."

"Mary Alice can barely walk," June agreed, then grinned when she saw he was wearing a large floppy straw hat in addition to his incredibly tasteless Hawaiian shirt.

"Cute," she said, pointing at the hat.

"Thanks." His smile was evil. "Don't you worry, girlie girl. Hannah told me to get enough hats for everyone. We're all supposed to wear them."

June frowned at him. "You're kidding."

His smile got big as he shook his head.

June rolled her eyes. "Oh, for God's sake."

"She insisted. I had to buy them, June. I hadda."

June shoved at him, and he laughed.

Unlike her, Deacon would do whatever Hannah asked. Too bad Hannah hadn't figured that out yet. Sometimes June just wanted to shake the girl. If a guy like Deacon Black had been interested in *her*, she'd have jumped him in a heartbeat.

Her smile faded. Well, once upon a time she'd thought a guy like him *had* been interested in her, hadn't she? Just went to show how wrong you could be.

So maybe she should keep her mouth shut.

"Hannah looks like a general getting ready to address the troops," Deacon commented beside her.

It was true. Hannah was pacing, hands clasped behind her back, a scowl of concentration on her face while the staff settled around the bar and waited for instructions.

Mary Alice and Grace Cooper, the third server, were sitting on bar stools next to June. Jason Nguyen, the part-time bartender, was behind the bar with Deacon getting glasses set up. He was wearing one of the floppy straw hats, but apparently it was too big because he kept pushing it back so he could see.

Kevin Barbet, the second chef, was standing at the kitchen door, massive arms crossed over his barrel chest, round face impassive. He was not wearing one of the hats, but his T-shirt was bright orange and said "Kiss Me – I'm From Haiti," complete with huge, red lips.

Billy Phillips, their worthless dishwasher, was slumped at the far end of the bar. Since he didn't smell like he'd showered in the recent past, June was glad he was that far away.

"We're having Bob's party tonight," Hannah said, as if they didn't know.

"Oh, it's just so awesome that you're having his party here, Hannah," Mary Alice gushed. Strands of her flyaway brown hair were floating gently around her plain face, and she had a flower the same red as her shirt tucked behind her ear. Her hands, as big as a truck driver's, were clasped at her chin, and her rather protuberant blue eyes were misty.

Hannah frowned. "Mary Alice—"

"I mean, how great is it that Bob's going to be a

missionary in Indonesia and help people and kids and everything? That's just wonderful. How old is he now, like seventy? And to leave his law firm and pick up and move to a whole other country? It's terrific." Mary Alice beamed her slightly insane smile.

Hannah looked uncomfortable. "Yeah, it's—"

"I can't wait to tell him how much I admire him," Mary Alice blinked wet eyes. "I wish my friend Candy was still in town so she could come to the party. Don't you think she would have liked Bob?"

June had met Candy on several occasions, and she was pretty sure the woman wouldn't have liked Bob all that much. Men didn't seem to be her thing.

"Where did Candy go anyway, Mary Alice? She hasn't been in for a while," Grace asked. The younger woman's gorgeous, mocha-colored skin glowed in contrast to the fuchsia leis she wore draped around her slender neck. She, too, had a flower tucked behind her ear into her neat cornrows, but hers was a brilliant pink to match the leis.

June wondered how Grace and Mary Alice would react when they saw the ugly straw hats Hannah wanted them to wear. That would be amusing.

"I don't really know where she went," Mary Alice admitted sadly. "She just told me she had to get out of town fast, and I probably wouldn't ever see her again."

Deacon, who had gotten himself some coffee, reached across the bar to pat Mary Alice's shoulder. June could see the liquid in his mug sloshing, as he struggled to control his laughter.

"*Any*way," Hannah said, "I think Bob told everyone he knew about this party. He wanted a really great send-off."

"I know he told everyone at the Rotary," Jason volunteered. He worked Friday and Saturday nights at the country club a few miles outside of town. The highfliers in the local Rotary

Club tended to hang out there to do their drinking, instead of coming into the Country Time.

"Right," Hannah said. "He deals with a lot of people from all kinds of backgrounds, so he wanted to have the party somewhere everyone would feel comfortable."

"And you told him you wouldn't charge him for having it here. The country club wanted him to pay for a room," Jason added helpfully.

Deacon snorted out a laugh. June thought some of his coffee might have come out his nose.

"Regardless—" Hannah said. She might have been clenching her teeth, but it was hard to tell. "I asked everyone to come into work because we're going to be packed."

"We knew that," June said, just to get Hannah even more riled up.

Hannah spun and pointed a finger at her. "We're going to give Bob the best party he's ever had, darn it. They're going to be talking about this for weeks. Months. Maybe years! When the history of Hardy Falls is written by Grace—"

Grace, who was an English major at the local university, ducked her head and blushed.

"—she will write pages about the excellent food, service, and beverages of this party. Right?" she snapped at Grace.

Grace straightened her shoulders. "Um, right."

"Good." Hannah nodded and glared at them. Her brown hair was pulled into a long, wavy ponytail that set off her sharp-boned face. June had seen women more beautiful than Hannah, but no one was more striking.

Of course, she might be a little biased.

"We have a chance to prove something here," Hannah said in all seriousness. "We can show everyone in town that we can pull off something special."

"And make a lot of money," June put in.

Hannah pointed at her again. "Bingo! The party officially

starts in a couple of hours, but I expect people to come in before that." She looked at June, Mary Alice, and Grace. "Will you guys be able to hang here in case we start table service early?"

Mary Alice and Grace agreed at once. June nodded. Hell, she didn't have anywhere else to be. If they weren't busy, she'd just sit at the bar.

"What about me?" Billy whined. "Can't I just come back later?"

Hannah rolled her eyes. "Fine." She looked at the rest of them. "So? Are we ready for Operation Bob?"

"As we'll ever be," June agreed.

It turned out Hannah was right about people coming early for the party. Even though it wasn't supposed to start until seven, Bob himself showed up before four. He was accompanied by Hannah's Uncle George, Mayor Ruffio, used car salesman Claude Beecher, and three other members of the Rotary. And that was just the beginning. People drifted in steadily as they got off work, and Hannah started table service by four thirty.

June didn't mind. She liked being busy. Besides, running around waiting on customers kept her from thinking about Calvin.

Which, of course, she wasn't going to do.

Except she sort of was.

Annoyed with herself, June frowned at the beer tap as she drew drafts for some regulars.

Would he come to the party tonight?

It fucking didn't matter what he did, she told herself. He could do whatever he wanted. Didn't mean a damn to her.

Walking back to the tables, she delivered the drafts to two guys who worked at a local factory and took their orders for burgers and fries back to Hannah and Kevin in the kitchen. Then she threw herself wholeheartedly into her work, focusing on getting food and drink orders, on talking, laughing, and joking with the customers. On acting normal.

Around eight, she was talking with Old Albert Cromwell and his friends, Joe Horton, Martin Scanner, and Harry Newman. The four old men were in almost every night, and she usually enjoyed hearing about their exploits.

Still laughing over Albert's story of how he'd taken Ms. Gregory out to see an extremely sexy thriller at a movie theater twenty miles away so they wouldn't be recognized, June noticed three men walking in the front door, all dressed in cheesy, lime-green striped bowling shirts.

Bernie Housemann, a siding contractor, and a total asshole, was in the lead. He swaggered into the room, smirking, eyes moving as he checked out the crowd. Chet Hinkle, an insurance salesman, was in the rear. He hiked up his pants and tried to straighten his bowling shirt over his round beer gut.

In the middle was Calvin Hardy.

3

Calvin followed Bernie Housemann into the Country Time and held the door open for Chet behind him.

He'd known Bernie and Chet since elementary school—thanks to their last names, the teachers had always seated them next to each other. They'd hung out as teenagers when they'd all been on the high school football team and had bowled together in a league before Calvin had left town. There'd been a time when he'd considered the other men to be close friends.

Which was just one more example of how stupid he'd been.

He wished he'd gone home after the bowling leagues like he usually did, but he'd let himself get talked into coming to Bob Johnson's party because he'd had the half-formed idea of thanking June for helping his mother that afternoon. He didn't expect her to appreciate the gesture, but maybe it could be the first step toward some kind of a truce between them. If he was going to be living in Hardy Falls again, he'd like to be on a more comfortable footing with her. The town was too small for them to avoid each other forever.

That's what he'd told himself, anyway.

Now, looking at the jostling crowd inside the Country Time,

he realized his timing was crap. Even if June would listen to him, which was highly unlikely, there was no way they'd be able to talk. So, he guessed he'd just grab a beer, and then hit the road.

Bernie glanced at him over his broad shoulder and grinned slyly.

"Place look any different, Cal?"

"No," Calvin said shortly, hoping to discourage further conversation.

"You haven't come drinking with us since you've been back," Chet said. "We were beginning to think you'd never set foot in the Country Time again."

"Yeah, Cal. Why's that?" Bernie grinned at him again, his smile saying he knew perfectly well why Calvin had been avoiding the place.

Calvin ignored him, or tried to. Chet was okay, but Bernie had always been a jerk. Still, Bernie was a siding contractor now, and Chet sold homeowner's insurance, which made them excellent referral sources for Hardy Hardware and Building Supply.

That was the only reason he'd gotten in touch with them when he'd moved back to town, and the reason he'd rejoined the bowling league, even though he'd known he'd have to see Pat Murphy, and that Pat used to date June. It was the reason he did a lot of things these days.

Yes, it was hard to look at Pat and know the guy used to touch June, kiss her, make love to her. But Calvin did what he had to do.

He shifted his shoulders, as the weight he always seemed to carry around pressed down harder.

His feelings didn't matter anyway. He'd thrown away any right he might have had to be upset when he'd dumped June and sped out of town in his souped-up convertible.

The only thing that mattered now—the only thing that

could matter—was the fact that bowling was the favorite pastime in Hardy Falls, and being in a league gave him excellent access to potential customers. A big-box superstore had opened a few miles outside of town, and since Calvin's father hadn't exactly been paying attention to the shop lately, Calvin had returned to find the foundations of his family's 140-year-old business crumbling around them. He needed as many contacts as he could get.

The noise was deafening as he followed Bernie through the Country Time's crowded taproom. That afternoon he'd been too focused on his mother, and then June, to notice much about his surroundings, but now he took a moment to look.

So much was the same. The same old wood paneling glowed smooth and golden, the same stained glass lanterns hung suspended over the same round or rectangular tables. Country music pounded through the speakers, as it always had. It could even have been the same Phillies game playing on the television, although the screen itself was flat and modern now.

But it was disorienting to realize he didn't recognize either of the bartenders. It felt strange to look around and not see Fred holding court at one of the tables, strange to know the man was dead and gone, and that the woman running this place hadn't even been in high school when Calvin had left town.

So much time wasted.

"Lots of people here," Bernie said proudly, as if he was responsible. "Bob'll be happy."

"Bob'll be happy because everyone'll buy him drinks," Chet put in.

Bernie honked out a laugh.

"Hey, maybe we'll get lucky, eh? Pick up a woman?" He elbowed Calvin in the stomach.

Calvin grunted noncommittally. He wasn't sure what alternate reality Bernie lived in. They were wearing striped bowling shirts, for Christ's sake. And picking up a woman wasn't high on his priority list these days anyway.

Well, unless it was…

He shook his head to dispel the thought and pushed his way up to the bar. One of the bartenders, a big guy wearing a straw hat and a Hawaiian shirt with an eye-searing pattern, shot him a grin and asked what he'd be drinking.

Calvin ordered a draft beer and took the glass when the bartender handed it to him. He paid for the drink then, sipping the beer, stood with his back to the bar and stilled.

There she was.

June was standing on the other side of the room, wearing one of those silly straw hats over her long, dark hair. Their eyes met, and Calvin drew in a deep breath.

She was so beautiful. So vital and alive. Talking to her that afternoon had made him feel like he was finally waking up after having been asleep for years.

His heart ached, a stark reminder of everything he'd thrown away.

But maybe they could be civil. Maybe he could show her that he'd changed.

Bernie elbowed him, and some of Calvin's beer sloshed onto his bowling shirt before he could tighten his grip on the glass.

"Well, lookee there, Cal." The other man indicated June with his chin.

Chet swiveled on his bar stool to see what they were looking at.

"It's June," he said stupidly.

"I think she saw you, Cal, cause there she goes." Bernie laughed as June nodded at one of the other servers and disappeared into the kitchen. Calvin waited, but she didn't come back.

"Oh, yeah. She saw you." Bernie laughed again.

"Shut up," Calvin muttered. He downed the rest of his beer in a few quick swallows, then turned to find the same bartender standing behind him, considering him with a flat, assessing stare.

"Need something?" the guy asked.

He needed June. He'd needed her almost as soon as he'd left her and shot what they'd had all to hell and back.

"Another beer," he said.

The bartender got him another draft. Calvin took it, paid, and sipped while he contemplated the kitchen door through which June had disappeared.

"June's on break," the bartender said. Calvin started because he hadn't realized he was still there. "I'm Deacon," the other man added and extended a hand over the bar.

"Calvin." Calvin took the offered hand and shook, amused by the tightness of Deacon's grip. He was even more amused when he found himself trying to match it. Dominance games. Next they'd be pissing a circle around the bar to mark their territory.

Deacon let go, and Calvin saw an answering glint of humor in the man's bright blue eyes before he pushed the floppy straw hat he wore further back on his head.

"June's my friend," he said, leaning on the bar. "I try to look out for her, yeah?"

"Good." Calvin studied his hard face and decided that, even though he held himself with an air of quiet confidence, he was probably only in his late twenties. "How long have you been working here?" he asked.

"A while. I started when I came back to town about two years ago." Deacon grinned. "You might not know me, but I've heard all about you. Just haven't been able to get down to the hardware store to introduce myself." He straightened when someone signaled him. "Be right back." He slid away, waited on some customers and helped a plump server with brown hair and a vacant expression mix drinks for her tables.

"Sorry," he said to Calvin when he got back. "Busy."

"Only to be expected," Calvin said, propping an elbow on the bar. "So, you said you've been 'back' two years? What's that mean? You lived here before?"

"Yeah. My family's here," Deacon said. "I've been gone, but it was time to come back."

"Huh." Calvin frowned, sifting through his memory and coming up blank. "I don't remember you."

Deacon shrugged. "You were already gone before we moved to town."

"Oh." Calvin sipped his beer. "So, do you think June is outside?" he asked, trying to sound casual. Unless things had changed, the Country Time staff had an area set up behind the building where they could take breaks away from the heat and the noise. If June had gone out there, he could talk to her without the whole town watching. Then if she smacked him in the face, nobody else would know.

He remembered that before he'd screwed everything up, talking hadn't exactly been on the agenda. He'd wait for June back behind the Country Time, and they'd spend her break making out in the cab of his truck, exchanging long, hot kisses until she'd had to run because she was late getting back.

Deacon looked wary. "I guess. Why?"

"I just need to see her for a minute."

Deacon didn't seem to like the idea, but he was called away to wait on more customers before he could comment.

Calvin put down his glass and moved to leave. This was his chance.

"Where are you going?" Chet asked, peering at him from the other side of Bernie.

"Just thinking I'd take off," Calvin told him. And he would, after he talked to June.

"Right," Bernie smirked at him.

Calvin turned away before he did something stupid, like plowing his fist into Bernie's smug face, but stopped abruptly when he found his path blocked by an extremely tipsy Bob Johnson, the man of the hour. The lawyer's blue eyes were already bloodshot, his silver mane of hair a disheveled mess. He'd lost his suit jacket at some point, and his shirt was unbuttoned far enough to show off more of his hairy chest than Calvin needed to see.

"How you boys doin'?" he asked, clasping Calvin and Bernie on their shoulders.

"We're fine, Bob," Calvin said, resigning himself to the delay. "It's a great party."

"Yeah," Chet agreed. "The whole town must be here."

"Well, I wanted to see everyone before I went away." Bob chuckled heartily. "Gimme another rum and coke, Deacon, wouldya?" he asked the bartender.

Deacon got the coffee pot and a mug, instead.

"How about we switch over to coffee for a bit, Bob, okay?" he asked jovially.

Bob's expression turned mulish. "Don't want coffee."

"Just for a while," Deacon soothed. "And maybe you could eat something too."

Bob frowned. "Got any of that peach pie around?"

Deacon smiled at him. "I'll check." He filled the mug with coffee and gave it to Bob, catching Calvin's eye as the lawyer started talking to Bernie. "Don't worry," he said quietly. "I've already got his keys. I'll get him home afterward."

"Good."

"So what the hell, Bob?" Bernie was asking loudly. "Indonesia? What the hell?"

"Yeah," Chet chimed in. "And a fucking missionary? Are you fucking kidding me?"

Chet's language tended to deteriorate as alcohol entered his bloodstream.

Bob took a slug of his coffee and looked sad. "Yeah, well, you know," he said vaguely.

Actually, Calvin didn't know. Bob had always been about as spiritual as a piece of plywood. He suspected bullshit.

"It is a great party, though," Bernie said, and belched, the scent of his beer breath wafting around them.

"Where else would I have had my goney...gooney...going away party?" Bob slurred. "Fred was a helluva friend. A helluva friend." His eyes grew damp. "I mish the hell outta him, I'm telling you the trush."

Calvin had always thought Fred was a bastard. On the other hand, he wasn't surprised Fred and Bob had been friends. Bob was a bastard, too.

Bernie hit Bob on the shoulder sympathetically. "But Fred's girl is carrying on, right? The Country Time's still here."

"Yesh," Bob agreed. "Hate to leave her. Been her lawyer since Fred died and wash Fred's lawyer before that. Hate to leave her..." he trailed off.

Calvin took a step away from the group. If he hurried, he could still catch June outside before her break was over.

Bernie elbowed Bob in the side. "Think you'll hook up with some island girl, Bobbie? Maybe find a lovely lady to set you up in her hut?"

Chet laughed. "I'd be looking to see if you can get one for the road." He took a long drink. "Must be somebody here who would screw you tonight."

Bob hoisted his bulk onto an empty bar stool. "Would be nice," he admitted wistfully.

"June's not with Pat anymore," Bernie said. "You should make a move on her."

Calvin froze. It was only when his hands started aching that he realized he'd clenched them into fists.

Chet snorted. "Yeah, even if June was willing, it's not like Pat's going to let anyone come near her. Man's severely territorial."

Bernie shot a look at Calvin and grinned. "Doesn't matter what Pat wants anymore, does it? They split up months ago. I say Bob should go for it."

Calvin willed himself not to pound Bernie's head into the bar. The other man lived to get other people stirred up.

"Pat says he doesn't believe they're really through," Chet insisted. "He was royally pissed when she broke it off. Keeps coming around trying to get her to realize she made a mistake."

Bernie just shrugged and took a large swallow of his beer. "Who wouldn't be pissed?" He elbowed Bob, and the older man practically fell off his bar stool.

Calvin forced his hands to relax but still struggled for control. Was Pat bothering June? Maybe he needed a little convincing to back off.

"Is Pat here?" he asked abruptly. He hadn't seen the other man in the crowd.

"Who?" Bob blinked at him. "Oh, Pat. Sure, he's here. He's my best friend in the whole wide world."

"Where is he?" Calvin snapped, some of his anger morphing into worry. June was probably alone.

"I dunno. Somewhere." Bob gestured widely with the hand holding his mug and coffee splashed all over Bernie like a tidal wave.

"Holy Christ!" Bernie cried, as the hot liquid hit him. He tried to leap to his feet, but his legs got tangled in the bar stool, and he fell back into Chet. Both men landed hard on the floor.

Calvin took advantage of the commotion that followed to slip away without anyone noticing.

He had to find June.

4

June sat slumped in one of the plastic Adirondack chairs they had set up out on an old cement pad behind the Country Time. It was a good place to get away from everything for a few minutes when you were working. Or to find refuge when your past seemed intent on knocking you on your ass every time you turned around.

Calvin.

Well, at least his mother hadn't shown up this time.

Crossing her arms over her chest, June sprawled in the chair and glared at the stand of scrub trees growing on the other side of the parking lot.

He'd looked tired.

She immediately pushed the thought away. What the hell did she care if Calvin looked worn down? She didn't give a crap if his face was drawn, his dark eyes sunken, his black hair threaded with silver.

Maybe she'd have gray hair, too, if she ever lost her mind and let it go natural. Neither one of them was as young as they used to be.

She still remembered the first time she'd seen him, all those years ago. She'd been twenty-two, working at the Country Time a couple of months, still debating whether or not she'd stay. Fred had been making moves on her, even after she'd made it clear she wasn't interested, and it had been really annoying. On top of that, she'd known damn right well people in town were talking about her behind her back, even though she hadn't done anything except work since she'd come to Hardy Falls.

But there'd been Hannah. Every time June had gotten fed up and decided it was time to hit the road again, there'd been Hannah. She hadn't been able to bring herself to leave the girl with the sad eyes. Kid's mama had died in a car crash when she was eleven, and now all she had was Fred, poor thing. June just couldn't bring herself to desert her, too. So she'd stayed.

Then, one night when she'd been waiting tables, flirting with some of the middle-aged bowlers, she'd turned to take a couple of orders to the kitchen and come face to face with... him. He'd been sitting at the bar, sipping from a bottle of beer —foot hooked up on the base of his bar stool, jeans stretched tight over his strong thighs. And he'd been watching her, dark eyes hot and intense.

Thinking about that look still made her shiver.

She'd wanted to run away.

Then he'd smiled at her, just a crook of full, sensual lips and she'd moved closer instead. Hell, she'd been lucky her knees hadn't buckled under the sudden wave of lust that washed through her.

She'd walked up to him, clutching the empty tray to her chest, and stopped a few feet away, just out of touching distance.

"Hi," she'd said.

His smile had broadened. "Hi."

"I'm June."

"I'm Calvin." He'd studied her. "Are you doing anything after you get off work?"

She'd shaken her head.

His dark eyes had glowed. "Good."

And that had been it. They'd started seeing each other, sleeping with each other, although, honestly, they hadn't actually slept all that much. She'd found out he was back in town after getting a graduate degree in architecture, was a descendant of the original founder of Hardy Falls, and that his family owned the local hardware store. Everyone knew him, everyone liked him.

Especially June.

She should have known it was too good to be true when, after they'd been seeing each other for a couple of weeks, he'd taken her to dinner at his parents' house. It had not gone well. She should have expected it, considering the fact that every time she'd come into contact with his mother in the past, Eva had treated her like garbage.

Sure enough, when she'd walked into the Hardys' graceful farmhouse with Calvin, his mother had sniffed and turned away. His father had been civil, but disapproval had flowed off the man in waves.

At the time, she hadn't cared what they thought. All that had mattered was Calvin.

And then he'd been gone.

"June."

The unexpected sound of her name jerked her from her thoughts. She straightened in the plastic chair and turned to see a man step out of the shadows and come striding towards her.

Pat. Great. As if the day couldn't get any better.

She stood and faced him, watching him walk. Even now, when she was irritated with him, she couldn't help but admire the way he looked in jeans and a black leather jacket. Pat's face would never grace the cover of a romance novel, but thanks to his obsessive dedication to his daily workouts, his body was a thing of sculpted beauty.

June was pretty sure what had convinced her to finally give in and start dating him in the first place hadn't been his persistence—she'd just wanted to get her hands on all that muscle.

Or maybe she'd wanted to get her hands on someone.

Pat stopped in front of her, and she eyed him warily.

"What are you doing here?" she demanded.

"I wanted to talk to you."

"There's nothing to say."

"I want to see you again, June." He reached out to her, but she pulled back to avoid the touch. He rubbed his fingers together, then let his hand drop.

"I think about you, baby," he rumbled, his voice deep gravel. "We were good together, you know we were."

June sighed and rolled her eyes heavenward. How many times did they have to go through this?

"It's over, Pat," she said. "Please do us both a favor and get that through your head." She tried to sound gentle and soothing, but it really wasn't one of her skills. Based on the way Pat's expression darkened, she was certain she hadn't pulled it off.

"That's what you say now, but you've changed your mind before," he said.

Damn it all! June liked to think she didn't screw up often, but when she did, it was usually a total clusterfuck.

She'd been with Pat over a year before she'd finally gotten up the energy to break it off six months ago. He hadn't liked it much but seemed to deal. Then, a few weeks later, she'd heard that Calvin would be moving back to Hardy Falls. The news had rocked her to the core.

For the first time since she was twenty-three, she'd thrown away all of her hard-won common sense. She'd just wanted to forget everything for one damned minute, wanted some freaking human comfort. So she'd gone to Pat, and he'd been ready, willing, and able to help her out. She'd regretted the night as soon as it was over.

And now the stubborn ass thought she was playing some kind of a game and refused to back off. June was confident that, considering his sexy body and healthy bank account, Pat didn't hear "no" very often.

The best part? That night hadn't done anything to make her feel better. Some things just stayed with you.

"Listen to me," she said, trying to hold onto her patience. "It's done."

"You came to me, remember? You seduced me back into bed," he said. "You were all over me, couldn't get enough of me."

"It was a mistake," she insisted.

"Stop saying that." Pat's homely face tightened. "You're just scared."

Scared? The man was driving her nuts. June pulled a hand through her hair then flung it wide. "I don't get this, Pat. I mean, what the fuck? Why are you so focused on me? You're only forty-four and totally jacked. You can get anyone you want. Just let it go."

"I want you." He crowded into her personal space.

"But I don't want you!" she shouted at him, far more forcefully than she'd intended.

He took another step toward her, the silver clasps on his leather jacket jingling, and gripped her shoulders in his hard hands.

"You're scared," he repeated. "You liked what we did in bed well enough. I know you miss me, too. That's what you said when you came back to me that night. That you want me as much as I want you."

See? June thought. Grandma Rose was right; no good ever came out of lying.

"Oh, for God's sake!" she said, whatever minimal amount of

tact she might have possessed evaporating under her total exasperation. "I was in a bad place that night, and I thought you could give me what I needed. I was wrong. We are finished. Understand?"

Pat looked like she'd stabbed him, and June wanted to curse him for making her feel guilty. Then he smiled, and it was ugly.

"I get it now. I know what this is about," he said.

"Okay. What do you think this about?" She twisted away from him and propped her hands on her hips, refusing to back down.

He laughed without humor. "Calvin's back in town. You're running after him again, just like you did before."

Her temper, always quick, rose again. "Oh, yeah?"

"Yeah. Think he'll give you another tumble, June? Think maybe he'll screw you for old time's sake before he dumps you again and heads for the hills?"

"You know what? Fuck you," she snapped.

Fury flooded his blunt wedge of a face.

"You think you're too good for me." Pat snarled the words. "Now you want to throw me away like some piece of trash. From where I'm standing, you're the one who should be tossed out in the garbage."

June braced herself, but he turned on his heel and stalked away.

"Damn," she murmured and lowered herself into the nearest chair, exhausted.

"That could have gone better," a new voice said from behind her.

June didn't bother to move. She knew who it was.

Calvin Hardy.

Perfect.

Silence hung suspended between them for one humming moment. Then she heard footsteps and Calvin came to stand in front of her, hands jammed into the pockets of his jeans, the lime stripes on his stupid bowling shirt almost fluorescent in the glow of the crackling floodlights.

"What are you doing here?" she asked tiredly. Because this was getting ridiculous. The universe was just fucking with her now.

Calvin shrugged. "I wanted to make sure you were okay."

And suddenly she was furious, because he hadn't given a damn whether or not she was okay for years. The force of her anger gave her new energy. She pushed to her feet and faced him, fists clenched.

"Really?" She let the sarcasm drip in her voice. "*You* want to make sure I'm okay. You." She sneered the word.

"Yes," he said stubbornly. "Me. Based on what I saw, it's a good thing I came to find you."

She glared at him. "That was a private conversation between Pat and me, and none of your business."

Calvin's eyebrows lowered into a scowl.

"He was totally pissed off, and he could have hurt you."

"He wouldn't hurt me, and you don't have any right to stalk me."

"I wasn't stalking you," he insisted. "Look, Bob said Pat was at the party, but he wasn't in the building. I knew you were on a break out back. I thought I'd come check on you. Sue me if I cared whether or not you were okay."

June's heart twisted in her chest. Cared. *Right.*

"I'm not your responsibility," she told him. "I can take care of my own little self just fine. I've been doing it for years."

To her surprise he smiled slightly, the creases in his cheeks outrageously appealing. "Christ, June, I know you can take care of yourself. Why do you think I waited to see what happened before I stepped in? I knew you'd rip me a new one if I tried to interfere before you needed help."

He was standing too close, looking at her too intensely. She couldn't breathe, couldn't talk to him after so much time. "I have to go," she said, hoping to hell he couldn't hear the desperation in her voice.

"Wait, there was another reason I came looking for you." He reached out a hand as if to grab her arm, but dropped it before he did. "I wanted to thank you for helping my mother this afternoon. That's why I came to the party—"

"Okay," she interrupted him, needing to be gone.

"No, I...see, we were across the street at the gas station. I only left her alone in the car for a minute to get her some candy and then...she wasn't there."

He ran a hand through his hair in a hauntingly familiar gesture. It was shorter now, well above his collar, where before it had been well below. June could remember how the thick strands had felt flowing between her fingers, like rumpled silk. He looked up, trapping her in the darkness of his eyes.

"Okay," she repeated with a gasp, the shaft of pain unexpected and intense. He was killing her. Fifteen years since he'd dumped her, and the feelings roaring through her made it seem like it happened yesterday. She was *such* an idiot.

"I have to get back," she said, and practically ran for the safety of the Country Time.

"June!" he called after her, but she didn't stop. Did not look back.

She shoved open the door and walked into the kitchen where Hannah and Kevin were working, while Billy, moving like a slug on sedatives, pretended to run the dishwasher. Hannah, brown hair stuffed under a baseball hat, chef apron liberally splashed with barbecue sauce, looked up from plating a burger and fries and smiled at June, lighting up like she always did. Something inside June settled a bit at the girl's obvious welcome.

"You missed the excitement," Hannah told her. "Apparently Bob threw coffee on Bernie, and there was some screaming. But Deacon said Bernie didn't really get burned."

"Couldn't happen to a nicer guy," June said absently. "I need you to do me a favor."

Hannah wiped her forehead with the back of her wrist. "Sure."

That was one of the things she loved the most about Hannah. No questions. No hesitation. Just, *sure*.

"Trade places with me," June said. Maybe she was a coward, but she couldn't go out into the taproom. Calvin might still be there, and she needed time to get her act together before she saw him again.

Hannah blinked. "Huh?"

"Trade places with me."

Now Hannah's eyes narrowed suspiciously. She drew off the thin latex gloves she was wearing for handling food and threw them away. "Why? Did Bob grab your ass?"

"You know I can't stand being politically correct, and all of the town big shots are out there," June said, improvising since Bob's roving hands were the least of her worries at the moment. "Besides, you're the fancy business owner. Get out there and work the party. Schmooze and network and all that shit."

"Don' let her fool you, boss lady," Kevin called. He was swaying to his own internal rhythm as he worked the grill. "She just wants to be in here with me, no?"

"Who wouldn't?" Hannah pinched his bicep, and Kevin let out his deep, rolling belly laugh.

"Come on, Hannah." June smiled, but she wasn't sure if she looked nonchalant or insane. "Take pity on me. The whole freaking Rotary's out there, including Claude Beecher. Do you really want me going after that smug bastard with a knife?" June had made the mistake of buying a used car from Beecher Auto Sales last year. The thing was a total lemon, and she'd been fighting with Claude for months.

Come to think of it, going after Claude with a knife might not be such a bad idea.

"Yeah, no. Don't do that." Hannah took off her dirty apron, wadded it up, and threw it toward the laundry bin. "You're sure?" she asked again, as she pulled off the ball cap.

"Yes. Go." Most nights, June wasn't thrilled about working in the kitchen. It was all heat and grease and the heavy smell of cooking meat. But at the moment, it was also a sanctuary.

She figured everyone deserved a sanctuary once in a while. Just for a few minutes.

"Okay." Hannah retied her ponytail. "Come get me when you change your mind." She stuck her tongue out at June and left the kitchen.

Relieved, June went to get a clean chef's apron. She pulled the strap over her head and started to knot the tie behind her back, but paused when she saw Kevin watching her.

"What?" she demanded.

He held up his hands, one clutching a spatula. "Nothin', nothin'."

June scowled at him and finished tying the apron. "The hell it's nothing."

Kevin just rolled his shoulders. "You don't like workin' in the kitchen all that much." He frowned. "And you look pale." Stepping up to her, he laid a beefy hand on her arm. "You need help? You want me to go out there and bash somebody's head for you?"

June touched his hand and then stepped away. Honest to God, if she started bawling she'd never forgive herself.

"I'm all right." She forced a smile. "Like I said, just tired of playing nice."

"Uh huh." Kevin looked skeptical.

"You'd better get to work." She pointed at the unfilled food orders stacked on the counter.

After another moment, Kevin nodded. "Okay." He turned back to the grill.

"Get moving, Billy," June called, not bothering to look at the boy. A minute later, the dishwasher roared to life, drowning out the sounds of the taproom. Mary Alice came bustling in with more food orders. Kevin gave her plates with burgers, chicken strips, wings, and hot dogs. June plated burgers, added sides, put together cold sandwiches, and set completed orders on the pick-up counter.

They fell into the routine. Grace, Mary Alice, and sometimes Hannah, walking in and out. Kevin and June working. Billy standing idle until somebody yelled at him. Everything was normal and safe and fine.

Sanctuary.

5

Calvin thought about heading home after his confrontation with June. He even walked around the building to where he'd left Big Red, his huge, fire-engine red pickup truck, sitting in the bowling alley parking lot.

He'd call it a night. No one would miss him if he didn't go back to the party. June obviously didn't want to talk to him, and he'd made the effort to thank her, which had been his excuse for showing up in the first place. He should just go. Game over.

Instead, he found himself pocketing his keys and walking back to the Country Time.

He'd hang out for a while to make sure Pat didn't bother June again. He'd seen the man's face when he'd walked away from her—she hadn't. Pat had been furious, and he wasn't known for clear thinking when he was in that state of mind.

Yes, there were plenty of other people around who'd step in and help if she was in trouble, but it couldn't hurt to have someone else watching out for her. Right?

Right.

Calvin pushed through the Country Time's front doors and

paused just inside the taproom, watching people talk and laugh while country music pounded in the air around them.

He was so full of shit.

The fact was, if Pat bothered June, and June didn't like it, she was more than capable of putting him in his place all by herself, as she had so ably demonstrated a few minutes ago.

So, why was he here again?

He didn't know.

Or maybe he did.

He stepped further into the room and saw Chet and Bernie sitting at a table with Bob Johnson, Claude Beecher, Hannah's Uncle George, and a couple of other guys he recognized as members of the Rotary. They were all talking and laughing, their voices loud above the music, their faces flushed in the low light. The front of Bernie's bowling shirt sported a huge, dark brown coffee stain, but as Calvin watched, he slapped Bob on the back and brayed with laughter. Apparently, all was forgiven.

Not wanting the group to notice him, Calvin edged around the crowd, got a cola from Deacon at the bar, and, rather miraculously, found an empty table tucked away in a corner. He slid behind it and sat with his back against the wall so he could watch the room. Taking a sip of soda, he sighed.

It had been a hell of a day.

The kitchen door opened and his heartbeat spiked, but it settled again when Hannah strode into the room instead of June. Hannah smiled at Deacon, then headed to where Bob was listing on his chair and propped him up. Soon she was working the room, talking and laughing with the customers, taking orders, and serving drinks.

Where was June? She should be back on shift by now.

Calvin contemplatively sipped his soda.

Well, Hannah had been stuck in the kitchen all night. She'd probably asked June to switch places with her for a while so she could come out and talk up the customers. That would be logical; something a business owner would want to do.

Except...hadn't June pretty much run away from him outside? And June never ran away from anything or anyone. Look at how she'd gotten all up in Pat's face. She couldn't be hiding. Could she? No, of course not. June never hid.

Did she?

Huh.

"How you doing, boy?"

Startled, Calvin blinked up at Albert Cromwell. The old man was standing next to the table, a wide grin deepening the lines in his weathered face, exposing his healthy pink gums. Old Albert didn't always bother to put in his teeth.

"I'm fine," Calvin gestured to an empty chair. "Want to sit for a minute?"

"Don't mind if I do." Albert pulled out the chair and sat, reed thin and graceful, despite the fact he had to have seen the back end of eighty a few years ago. He was also, as he was quick to point out, still in full control of his bodily functions. The older women in town seemed to appreciate the fact, and Albert was never at a loss for company if he wanted it.

"Where's your posse? Did they go home already?" Calvin asked. When Albert wasn't with a woman, he was almost always with his friends, Harry Newman, Joe Horton, and Martin Scanner. The four men tended to travel in a pack, like an elderly gang.

"Harry had to get back to his wife, 'cause she don't trust him when he goes to a party." Albert snorted in disgust. "What the hell does the fool woman think is going to happen? If she ever left her house, she'd know Harry wouldn't attract the attention of a blind flea, let alone another woman. Martin can't hold his liquor, so he was already done for the night, and since Joe was driving them both, he left, too." Another snort as Albert held up his glass, the amber liquid in it sparkling under the multicolored light of the stained glass lantern hanging over the table. "Lightweight. Person should stick with beer if he can't handle anything stronger."

"Right." Calvin considered the old man, saw he was flushed and just a wee bit unsteady. "And how are you planning on getting home there, buddy?" If Albert said he was driving, Calvin would have to tackle him for his keys. The man was enough of a menace on the road when he was sober.

"Don't you worry none about me," Old Albert leered good-naturedly. "That Mathilda Gregory's taking me back to her place tonight."

Calvin could see Ms. Gregory sitting with some other women on the far side of the room, her thin mouth pursed in a prim line. She'd been the town librarian for as long as he could remember, and she had always seemed to be about a hundred years old. Maybe she was preserved in formaldehyde or something.

On the other hand, he hadn't been all that surprised to learn the woman had started an online newspaper when the last local print paper had closed. She also owned a number of rental properties around town and was rumored to have acquired quite a sizable investment portfolio. Those sharp, dark eyes of hers reminded him of a hawk. Or a shark.

Albert winked at him. "Don't let the fact she's the librarian fool you. The woman does a lot of yoga. Makes things mighty interesting. She can put her foot behind her head."

"Ah." Calvin took a sip of his cola and devoutly wished he could burn that image out of his mind.

The old man cackled, then put down his drink and folded his arms on the table in front of him.

"So, how's your Ma doing?" he asked, sympathy replacing humor in his blue eyes.

Calvin shifted on the hard wooden chair.

"She's okay." He shrugged and put his glass on the table,

tried to line it up exactly with the corner. "Worse," he admitted after a moment.

"That's a damned shame." Albert sighed and settled back, his bony shoulders slumping. "A damned shame."

"Yeah," Calvin said, just to say something.

"How's your Pa doin'? Last time I saw him, he looked like hell."

"He seems better. With me here, he can get some rest, at least. We take turns watching Mom." Although it was becoming harder, as his mother's earlier adventure proved.

He hated the idea, but maybe it was time to consider putting her in a facility. They already had home health aides coming in every morning to help with personal care, but maybe there was enough money to swing someone coming more hours? Would that agitate his mother?

Calvin ran a hand distractedly through his hair, trying to dislodge the worries. "I just wish Dad had told me he was having problems sooner," he said to Albert. "We could have been talking, gotten a plan together, instead of scrambling around trying to figure out what to do."

Albert shook his head. "Man has his pride, son."

"Stubborn idiot," Calvin grumbled. But guilt burned in his gut all the same. He took a sip of soda to try to wash it away, without success.

He should have paid more attention to what was happening with his parents, but he'd been living in Philadelphia and hadn't made the trip home very often. Then his divorce from his wife, Kimberly, had turned into one of the more dramatic and bloody Wagnerian operas, consuming his life for over a year. He'd known about his mother's Alzheimer's, of course, but he hadn't realized how bad she'd gotten until the phone call telling him that his father had collapsed in the "nuts and bolts" aisle of Hardy Hardware and was in the hospital, at the point of utter exhaustion.

Calvin had dropped everything and rushed home. Sitting at his father's bedside, in a hospital room that smelled like antiseptic and bleach, he'd demanded to know why the *hell* the man hadn't told him he needed help before this. If he couldn't have come home, he would have called his aunts or cousins. None of the extended family lived in Hardy Falls anymore, having scattered around the country over the years, but surely they could have worked something out.

"I didn't want to bother anyone," his dad had said, calm as could be, totally ignoring the fact that his formerly massive body seemed whittled down to nothing under the white sheets of his narrow hospital bed. "I had it under control."

Riiiiiight. Because having it "under control" meant you were now on anti-anxiety medication, as well as two kinds of high blood pressure pills. Jesus.

"So, how's the hardware store going?" Albert asked. "It seemed kind of busy when I was there with Joe." Albert's friend, Joe Horton, repaired air conditioners during the summer and was always coming into the store for something or other.

"Better. Dad thinks we're turning things around." Calvin suspected it had been the fate of Hardy Hardware—not his own health—that finally pushed his father to the point where he'd been willing to accept help from his son.

Albert nodded his head. "Good, that's good." He picked up his drink and was quiet for a long moment, sipping before he put the glass back on the table. "I've always liked you, boy," the old man said at last.

"I've always liked you, too, sir," Calvin replied, truthfully. After Albert's beloved wife, Mabel, had died of cancer, and before he'd finally given up trying to keep his farm, Albert had worked nights at the hardware store, struggling to pay off medical bills.

Looking back, Calvin couldn't even begin to imagine how

difficult it must have been for the man to try and keep a farm going, work part time as a cashier, and deal with the unutterable grief of losing a spouse on top of it all. But Albert had always been patient, even when Calvin had whined about being forced to stock shelves after school.

"I've always liked you," Albert repeated, then shook his head. "But what you did to June? I didn't like that much."

Calvin stared down at his hands, at the thick fingers and chapped knuckles.

They were his father's hands. His grandfather's.

"I know," he said. There was no excuse for what he'd done to June. He'd dumped her with no reason, no room for argument. No care.

When he looked up again, he found the old man watching him intently.

"I reckon you listened to your friends, and maybe your family," Albert said. "Maybe you even believed some of the talk going around town about her."

Calvin swallowed. "I made a mistake."

He'd figured that out years ago, after he'd married Kimberly and the reality of what he'd done, what he'd thrown away, had finally begun to sink in. But by then he'd made a commitment to another woman, and he'd been sure June had moved on. It was too late to change anything.

His father wasn't the only idiot in the Hardy family.

Albert's expression was sympathetic. "I know how it goes. My mama didn't like my Mabel, same as yours doesn't like June. Mabel was Catholic, and that was enough to put my parents through the roof, even though it's a stupid reason not to like somebody. My friends made fun of her because her family was from Poland and she'd been raised with some old-fashioned ways. Me? I liked her just fine, but..." He shrugged. "I listened to them for a time, and I hurt her before I got my head out of my ass and begged her to forgive me. I know how easy it is to act like an imbecile because you think you're hot shit."

"Yes." It was easy to believe what people told you.

"You hurt June badly, boy," Albert said. "You almost broke her, and she's not a woman who breaks easily."

"No, she's not."

Everything inside Calvin felt hollow and empty. He'd just been kidding himself, coming here. Another mistake. He should have gone home after leagues, not tried to talk to her, not tried to see her one more time. He'd hurt her, he'd left her, and how could she ever forgive him?

She couldn't.

Sighing, he drained the last of his cola and pushed aside the empty glass, bracing his hands on the table to shove to his feet.

Albert reached over and grabbed his arm.

"Now don't go running off," he said unexpectedly, patting Calvin's arm paternally as he let go. "Yeah, you screwed up. After you left, June, well, she changed. Closed herself off. Maybe she kept company with Pat Murphy for a while, and perhaps one or two before him, but she was...colder. Hell, for a while there I got frostbite whenever she served me a drink. The only time she laughed was with Hannah. But she's been different since you've been back."

Calvin looked at the old man, curious in spite of himself. "Different how?"

Albert shrugged. "I can't explain it. Brighter, maybe? I wasn't sure how I felt about that, but you moving back home is the first thing that's really gotten under her skin in years. I haven't seen her this worked up since you left. I think it's good."

Calvin felt something a little bit like hope unfurl in that dark, empty place inside him.

"I'd like to make it up to her," he told Albert, leaning forward. "Walking away from her was the worst thing I've ever done." He stopped talking. The explanations belonged to June, if she'd listen.

Albert studied him, then nodded. "Well, it ain't gonna be easy, son. You're gonna need to keep her off balance because otherwise she's way too stubborn to listen to you. And you'd better buy a stainless steel jock strap because she's gonna twist your balls clear off."

Calvin smiled. For the first time since he'd moved back home—for the first time in years—the smile felt real.

"I know," he said.

Albert returned the smile, his own fierce. "If you hurt her again, I'll be coming after you with my shotgun. Both barrels."

Calvin swallowed. "Yes, sir."

"All righty then." The old man pushed himself to his feet and hiked up his khaki work trousers. "Now, I'm gonna go see if Mathilda's ready to leave so we can go to her place and check each other out. Get it?" He waggled his bushy eyebrows suggestively.

"Got it." Calvin tried to hide his wince at another image he could have done without. "Have fun."

Albert cackled. "You take care now." He waved and walked away.

Calvin watched him go, mind racing. If the old man was right, and Calvin's return to Hardy Falls had June "worked up," then maybe she wasn't completely indifferent to him. Maybe there was still a chance...

The kitchen door snapped open, and June marched into the room, driving his thoughts right out of his head. Her dark hair was swinging, her dark eyes were snapping, and she ostentatiously ignored the corner where he was sitting, her nose so high in the air he was sure she'd already spotted him.

Moving to Hannah with fierce purpose, June jerked a thumb toward the kitchen door, apparently telling the girl to take a break. There was a brief argument before Hannah sighed, then left with a shrug and a smile.

Calvin focused on June, watched her walk around the room. Watched her ignore him.

Oh, yeah. She was nervous.

He ordered another cola from the plump server with the wild hair and wide blue eyes, then settled back in his chair. His mother had been worn out, so his father shouldn't need him. There was no reason why he had to rush home. He could stick around until June got off her shift. Watch out for her.

Make her nervous.

His smile broadened. Maybe things were finally looking up.

6

June had spotted Calvin sitting alone at a table in the corner as soon as she'd left the kitchen to relieve Hannah for a break, so she'd known which part of the taproom to ignore while she was out there. But when she was heading back after Hannah returned, she made the mistake of looking directly at him. He smiled at her, as if he knew his mere presence wrecked her self-confidence.

Damn him! June slammed through the kitchen door, grabbed an apron, and jerked it over her head. Kevin looked up with surprise at the force of her entrance but backed off when she growled at him.

Why was Calvin still there? Why couldn't he have just gone home? Why couldn't he have dumped his mother in a nursing home and stayed in Philadelphia so she'd never have to see him again?

Well, screw him.

She yanked open a bag of frozen fries, emptied the contents into the fryer basket, and lowered the whole thing into hot oil, satisfied with the resulting cloud of steam and the sharp hissing sound.

Then she sighed.

And screw her, too, because she knew she would not be offering to cover for Mary Alice and Grace when it was time for their breaks. She would stay in the kitchen like a coward, and let the rest of them pick up the slack out front, just because she didn't want to face him again. At least not tonight.

Hannah had told them that the party would be over at midnight, but it was closer to one in the morning when she cut off food service. From the chorus of loud groans out front, Bob and his friends were disappointed, but June was glad. Now she could go home, take a shower to wash off the overpowering scent of cooked meat and fried oil, and fall into bed. She was exhausted, both physically and mentally. After a good night's sleep, she'd be able to put things in perspective, get back to normal.

Was Calvin still out in the taproom?

Well, she sure wasn't going to look. Anyway, he'd probably left a long time ago.

Frowning, she moved mechanically, helping Kevin with the cleanup chores. Once everything was basically in order, she grabbed her bag and her denim jacket, and made a break for it, pausing only long enough to take her share of the tip money and acknowledge the cheerful farewells of Grace and Mary Alice.

A few minutes later she was free, barreling down the highway in the piece of shit sedan she'd bought from Claude, heading home to her tiny apartment over Mathilda Gregory's garage—driving away from Calvin.

Her hands tightened on the wheel.

Okay, it was true that hiding in the kitchen for almost the whole night made her a freaking idiot, but she'd just needed a chance to adjust. She should have been more immune to Calvin after all this time, but she'd deal. When she saw him again, she'd be able to treat him like he didn't matter. Because he didn't.

Distracted by her thoughts, she didn't see the red light blinking on the car's dashboard until she was almost halfway home. When it finally caught her attention, she realized it was the battery light.

The battery light.

What did that mean again?

The battery light meant her car's electrical system...was...

June stared at the little light.

It stared back at her.

The battery light meant her car's electrical system was totally fucked, that's what that light meant.

A wave of anger crashed through her, chasing away the remaining exhaustion.

Son of a bitch! Son of a goddamned bitch!

Okay, okay. She tried to calm herself. This didn't have to be something horrible. Maybe the light had just short-circuited. That happened sometimes, didn't it? Or maybe it had been set off by a bad computer chip or something.

Or maybe the freaking alternator had crapped out. And considering her luck lately, she wouldn't be at all surprised if whatever was wrong was the most expensive option possible.

Jesus, this car had been nothing more than a rolling money pit since the day she'd bought it. Last month, she'd had to replace all of the hub mounts. Before that, she'd needed front *and* rear brakes. Before that, it had been the tires. And the muffler. Now this, whatever the hell "this" was.

Every time something happened, she called Claude. Every time, he sounded sad and said the needed repairs were considered "normal" and "expected," so the warranty she'd bought—another mistake—wouldn't cover them.

She wanted to take that warranty and shove it up the old bastard's ass so far he'd be able to read it without his glasses.

But first, she had to get home.

June willed the sedan to keep moving. Even if this was the worst case scenario, and the alternator had died, the engine would run on the battery for a while, wouldn't it? Just another six or seven more miles...

No sooner had the thought crossed her mind, the car lost power. No engine, no lights, no power steering or brakes. Nada. Zilch.

Because that was just the way her life was going.

Cursing fluently, she used the car's momentum to guide it to the shoulder and bring it to a stop. Without much hope, she put it in park, turned it off, and tried to restart it.

The engine made a sick sound, then fell into silence.

"Goddamn it!" June slammed the flat of her hand on the steering wheel and screamed in frustration at the top of her lungs. Because, why the hell not? It wasn't like there was anyone around to hear her.

The moon wasn't out, and there weren't any streetlights on this section of the road—naturally—so the inside of the car was darker than Satan's armpit. After a few deep breaths to get herself under some semblance of control, she groped for the glove compartment, opened it, and dug around for her flashlight. Eventually she found it and, with some trepidation, flipped the switch. A narrow beam of light shone in the darkness.

Halle-freaking-lujah. Something had actually gone right.

Not wanting to waste the batteries, June turned the flashlight off again and pulled her purse into her lap. Working by touch, she started searching for her cell phone.

Honest to God. Almost two fucking o'clock in the morning, and now she was going to have to call someone to come rescue her. And that was assuming she could get a cell signal, which could be kind of hit-or-miss around here. She was so going to roast Claude on a spit the next time she saw him. Slowly. With an apple in his mouth.

What made her the angriest was knowing this whole situation was her own fault. She should never have bought a car from Claude Beecher. He was practically the walking stereotype of a slimy, used car salesman. But he'd made it sound like he was giving her such a good deal that she'd fallen for his lines, and now she was stuck. After all, it wasn't like she could afford to just waltz out and buy another car.

She finally found her cell phone at the bottom of her purse, pulled it out, and hit the power button.

The screen stayed blank.

Heart pounding, she turned on the flashlight and shined the light on the phone to make sure she was hitting the right button before she pushed it again.

Nothing.

Clutching the lifeless phone in one hand and the flashlight in the other, June let her head fall back against the headrest and closed her eyes.

Of course the phone was dead. Why not?

Unable to help herself, she started laughing. Seriously, what else could you do when life got so ridiculous? She laughed even harder when the flashlight flickered and died, plunging the car back into darkness.

Priceless.

Suddenly, she heard the hum of another vehicle on the deserted highway. Headlights shone in her rearview mirror as it crested the hill behind her.

For about half a second, she debated getting out and trying to flag down the other driver, but quickly tossed the idea aside. Yes, it might be her only chance to avoid either spending the rest of the night in the car or walking six miles to get home, but with the way her day was going, she didn't want to risk it. Her sedan, her cell phone, and her flashlight might all be dead, but she preferred not to join them, thank you very much. With her luck, she'd get picked up by a bunch of zombies looking for late night takeout.

In the end, it didn't matter what she wanted because the other vehicle slowed down and pulled up behind her, headlights bright and blinding after the darkness. Obviously, the driver had seen her sitting in the car and was coming to check things out. June put up a hand to shield her eyes and clutched the flashlight tighter, ready to use the thing as a weapon if this person did indeed turn out to be a zombie instead of a Good Samaritan.

Through her side mirror, she saw the driver's door of the other vehicle—a pickup truck—open and a man get out. She couldn't make out any of his features, just a dark silhouette as he walked up to her door.

He bent down to look in her window.

"June? Are you okay?" Calvin Hardy asked.

June closed her eyes and tried not to start laughing again.

"Did your car break down?" he asked, his voice muffled through the window glass.

She glared at him, then threw the cell phone, flashlight, and purse onto the passenger seat and shoved open her door, forcing him to take a couple of steps back to make enough room for her to get out.

"No," she said with bitter sarcasm, as she slammed the door shut behind her, "I thought I'd stop here by the side of the road and look at the stars. Of course my car broke down." Her lip curled in disgust, and she turned her glare on the sedan. "I'm surprised the axle hasn't fallen off this hunk of junk yet."

Calvin tucked his hands into the front pockets of his jeans. "Okay, so what's wrong with it?" he asked.

"You mean, what's wrong with it *this* time?" June shrugged because he was here, so he might as well help. "The battery light came on before the car died, so it's probably the alternator. Hell, for all I know, it's the whole damn electrical system. I thought I might be able to make it home on the battery power, but that gave out, big shock." She took a deep breath, but the frustration welled up inside her again. "I can't freaking believe this! I've only had the thing a year!"

That last part might have come out as a wail, but June told herself she didn't care. A woman could only take so much before she snapped.

"Yeah? Who'd you buy it from?" Calvin asked idly, looking over the car in the light from his headlights, his face in shadow.

June shuffled her feet, feeling stupid and hating it. "Claude Beecher," she admitted reluctantly.

He snapped his head around to stare at her, mouth dropping open.

"Claude? Are you insane? Why in the hell did you buy a car from him?"

"Because I thought he was giving me a good deal." She kicked the front tire hard enough to hurt her foot through her cowboy boot. "Piece of garbage."

"Christ, June, he probably got it from a chop shop in Scranton. Did the title go through?"

June frowned at him, cocked out her hip and fisted her hand on it.

"Of course it did. What do you take me for?"

He shook his head and turned away. "Let me get a flashlight."

Her frown deepened as she watched him walk to his pickup and open the tailgate. "Why?"

Calvin got something from a toolbox bolted inside the bed of the truck. "Because I want to do a root canal." He turned on a powerful flashlight and came back to her. "Why the hell do you think? I want to take a look at your engine."

"Do you have an alternator in your pickup?" she demanded, following him to the front of her car and helping him raise the hood. "Because if you don't, you're not going to be able to do anything about it."

"Well sue me if I want to look."

"I bet you don't even know what you're looking at," she groused, standing beside him as he shone the beam of the flashlight into the engine compartment.

"I'm pretty sure I see metal."

June rolled her eyes heavenward. "Okay, smart guy. Tell me you also see a loose wire or something you can pop back into place, and I'll be on my way."

He didn't even bother dignifying that with a response as he bent over to study the engine. Since he was distracted, June gave herself permission to actually look at him. Such a strong profile. Arrogant nose. Arrogant man.

Or he had been, once upon a time.

He turned his head unexpectedly, eyes locking with hers before she could look away. June drew in a sharp breath, smelled the remains of his aftershave, the slight tang of sweat.

She drew back abruptly and took a few steps away from the car.

"Well?" she asked, sounding annoyingly breathless.

He studied her without moving, one hand braced on the frame of the car. Then he slowly straightened, and she was reminded how tall and broad he was. His smile was wicked.

"No loose wire. Sorry. Did you already call the tow truck?"

"Um." She shifted from foot to foot. "No."

"Okay." He nodded. "Let's try to jump the car first. Then you can call, if it doesn't work."

June winced. "I kind of forgot to charge up my cell," she admitted. "Maybe I can borrow yours to call Wally?"

"What the hell, June!" The lingering sexy smile immediately changed to exasperation. "If you're driving home alone in the middle of the night, you need to have a fully charged cell phone. Especially if you bought a car from Claude."

June's temper flared. "I was handling it."

"Bullshit. What would you have done if I hadn't come along?"

"I would have walked home like I'm still going to."

"Oh, for...don't be even more of an idiot," he growled at her. "We'll try to jump the car. If it starts and the battery holds a charge, I'll follow you home. If not, we'll use my cell to call Wally's garage, and I'll *take* you home."

A tiny rational part of her mind agreed that the plan made sense, but June wasn't in the mood to listen to it.

"Fine. You can call Wally's garage for me. Thank you. But then you can just take off. I'll catch a ride with the tow truck driver if the car doesn't start."

"June, use your head." He returned her glare. "I am sure as hell not going to leave you alone by the side of the road in the middle of the night with a broken-down car, waiting for a tow."

"Why not?" She sneered the words but stopped herself before she added the rest.

You left me alone before.

She might not have said it out loud, but Calvin seemed to hear her anyway. His expression hardened before he went back to his truck and began rummaging in the toolbox again.

"Let's see if we can jump your car," he said.

"I told you—"

"And I told you that I'm not leaving you alone," he snapped at her. "Have you even thought about the fact that Richie will be driving the tow truck at this time of night?"

"Oh." Wallace Dunlop, the man who owned the garage, was a great guy and a good mechanic. In fact, the worst thing she could say about Wally was that he let his brother, Richie, work for him, running the overnight towing business.

She tried to stay out of Richie's way. He was a racist pig who'd been on her back ever since she'd gotten in his face and barred him from the Country Time after he'd made Grace cry.

Besides, there were some good reasons why women living in and around Hardy Falls didn't call for a tow truck at night unless they had no other option. No way was June going to be alone with Richie.

She sighed. She was neatly boxed in. Calvin wouldn't let her walk home, and she couldn't take the tow truck.

"All right," she said, defeated. "You win."

Calvin nodded. "I know."

7

June watched Calvin rummage around in the toolbox in the bed of his truck. Finally, he pulled out some cables, shut the toolbox and the tailgate, climbed into the pickup, and drove it around to face her sedan, nose to nose.

The headlights blinded her, and by the time she could see again, he'd already opened the truck's hood, clamped one end of the jumper cables to its battery, and was busy fixing the other end to hers.

"Get in and see if the car starts," he told her.

This was a waste of time, but June didn't bother arguing. She obediently got into her sedan and turned the key. There was a whining noise, but the engine didn't turn over. Calvin shouted for her to try again, so she did. Then, because he was a man, he came and helped her out of the car, got behind the wheel himself, and tried to start it. Nothing.

"Well?" she demanded when he climbed back out, although the verdict was pretty obvious.

Calvin shook his head, took off the jumper cables, closed the hoods of both vehicles, and walked around the side of his truck to stow the cables. When all that was done, he came back to her.

"No good," he said, unnecessarily.

June crossed her arms and smirked. "Golly, really? It's almost like I knew what I was talking about."

He shot her a glare, opened the truck's passenger door, and ducked inside to grab a sleek cell phone.

"Come on, admit I was right," June prodded.

Calvin ignored her and flipped through the cell's directory, then hit a button and held it up to his ear. She listened while he made arrangements for Richie Dunlop to come tow her car. He even gave the other man the freaking mile-marker where she'd broken down.

After he'd hung up, he tucked the cell phone into the pocket of his lime-green striped bowling shirt and crossed his arms in a mirror of her stance.

"You were right," he said.

"Hah!" June crowed.

"The battery's completely shot. From what you've told me, the alternator's probably trashed, too. Satisfied?"

Well, not really. June sobered. Replacing the alternator was going to be expensive, not to mention the cost of the emergency tow. There went all of the money she'd been saving to buy the fancy digital camera she'd been wanting for ages.

"Thanks for calling Richie." She hesitated. "And thanks for staying." Because as much as she hated to admit it, she was glad he was there.

He snorted. "Like I'd just drive off. Please."

June smiled. "Well, thanks anyway."

They stood in awkward silence for a moment before Calvin shifted and dropped his hands to his sides.

"Do you, uh, want to sit in my truck while we wait? You know Richie. It's going to take him a while to get out here, and Big Red is comfortable."

She stared at him. "You actually named your truck?"

"Yeah. Some people name their cars, I named my truck." He sounded defensive. "Want to get in it?"

June considered the question. She wasn't all that anxious to be alone with Calvin in a confined space, especially since being with him in the front seat of a pickup truck brought back some memories she'd rather forget. They'd had some pretty good times parked in dark places, away from prying eyes.

On the other hand, she was already alone with him. And it *was* chilly. Might as well be comfortable.

"Okay," she said.

She got her purse out of the car, tucking the dead cell phone in her pocket and putting the dead flashlight back in the glove compartment. Then she went with Calvin to the pickup. He held open the door so she could climb into the passenger seat, closed it behind her, and walked around to jump up behind the wheel.

He didn't say anything, just fiddled with the heater a bit, and put on the hazard lights to blink yellow across the hood of her piece-of-shit sedan.

"Was your mother all right after you got her home?" June asked when she couldn't stand the silence any longer.

Calvin shrugged.

"She was all right when I left for the bowling league. Sleeping."

"Good." She glanced at him and found him watching her, eyes intent on her face.

He looked away.

"You were...kind to her," he said. "And maybe you didn't have a reason to be."

June didn't answer, just stared through the front windshield at the flashing lights.

Eva had never liked her. That one time Calvin had taken her to dinner at his parents' house, his mother had made little, cutting remarks through the whole meal, until June wanted to stab her in the eye with a salad fork.

It had been typical of her interactions with the older woman. Eva made chilly, pointed comments, and June tried not to hit her. After Calvin had dumped her and left town, June had seen the smug satisfaction on his mother's patrician face. She had *known* she'd done something to convince her son to go.

Fortunately, a few months after Calvin had left, Eva stopped coming into the Country Time. After that, June had gone out of her way to ensure she never ran into the woman again. It had mostly worked.

Still...

"She never treated me right," June murmured, "but how could I kick at her when she didn't even know me?"

"No, she doesn't know a lot of people these days. Even her sister doesn't bother coming from New York to visit anymore." Calvin ran his hands over the steering wheel. "But I still wanted to thank you."

She shrugged, feeling uncomfortable. "Sure."

"Right," he muttered and ran his hands over the wheel again. She wished he'd stop doing that. It made her think about how those hands had felt on her body, big and sure and calloused.

She drew in a deep breath and forced herself to look away, out at the empty road. Nobody had passed them since Calvin had stopped.

"How did you happen to come across me anyway?" she asked him with sudden suspicion. "You weren't following me, were you?"

He frowned at her. "No, I wasn't following you. But I would have been if I'd had the slightest idea you were driving a wreck of a car in the middle of the night without a working cell phone."

"Would you lay off about the cell phone?" June snapped. "If

you weren't following me, why are you even here? It's not like a lot of people use this road at this time of night." Obviously.

"I was going home. In case you've forgotten, it's the fastest way out to my parents' house."

"Oh, right." She had forgotten, actually.

"I saw a car sitting here and thought I'd see if I could help, if that's okay with you."

She sneered at him, not ready to let him know she was grateful.

"I don't need you looking out for me, Calvin. I've been taking care of myself for a long time."

He started to reply, then stopped when, as if conjured by the conversation, another set of headlights broke the darkness beyond June's car. A moment later, a pickup truck slowed to a stop beside them.

Calvin used his controls to lower the passenger side window. The driver of the other truck rolled down his window, and June saw Bernie Housemann. He looked surprised, then grinned knowingly.

She settled back with a groan. Of course. Why shouldn't the first person to come along in at least twenty minutes be Bernie Housemann?

"Hey, Cal," the other man called. "It's you, huh? Need any help? I saw the hazards." He leered at June. "Don't want to interrupt nothing."

"We're good, thanks," Calvin said, his voice frigid. "Just waiting for Richie to come tow June's car. Should you be driving?"

"I'm fine." Bernie brayed out one of his donkey laughs. "Deacon filled me up with coffee, and Hannah made me take a drunk test. Did you know she bought one of those breathawhatchamacallit things special for Bob's party? But I was okay. Only had a couple of beers. Knew I'd be driving. Anyways..." he trailed off, as his smile grew, "you two have fun."

"Sure." Calvin raised the passenger window as Bernie drove away, tires spitting gravel. "Sorry," he said, glancing at June. "Bernie's the biggest gossip in town."

"You think I don't know that?" June sighed. "And he's an asshole," she added.

"Yeah."

"I was kind of surprised to see you hanging out with him," she admitted. Even back when they were younger, she'd never understood why Calvin gave Bernie the time of day. The other man had always been a dick.

He shrugged. "Bernie's a siding contractor. He refers business to the store."

"I hope it's worth it."

"Me, too."

They sat silent, both of them staring out at the blinking hazard lights.

It was strange to be next to this man again, June thought. There'd been a time when she'd assumed they were inseparable. But she'd been wrong, hadn't she?

"Are you finally divorced?" she asked, to remind herself they weren't the people they'd been.

He shifted and turned to her. "I am."

"How's Kimberly taking it?" She knew his wife's name. Just like she knew he'd gotten married a year after he'd left Hardy Falls, and that his wife was a socialite from Bryn Mawr whose father was a partner in the high-class architectural design firm where Calvin had worked.

"I have absolutely no idea. I haven't spoken to her in months," Calvin said. "Our attorneys were handling everything. She wanted the house and higher alimony." His voice thickened with resentment. "No, I should say she wanted it all. She wanted everything I had worked for. She even wanted the business I started after her father fired me for wanting to divorce his princess."

June stared at him. "They fired you?" As far as she'd known, he'd been one of the firm's rising stars.

"Yes." His grin was sharp in the dim light. "So, I started a rival company."

"Good for you."

Calvin shook his head. "I hated it. The divorce and the business competition. I realized they were turning me into someone I didn't want to be. When I found out what was happening with my parents, I knew the only thing keeping me in Philly was pride. Just stupid pride."

He sounded sad and maybe angry with himself. June was sorry she'd brought up the subject of his bitch of a wife. Before she thought better of it, she reached out and wrapped her hand around his forearm. Since the bowling shirt had short sleeves, she touched his skin for the first time in years, felt the power of his muscles and tendons, his warmth tingling along her fingers.

He jerked slightly and then went still under her palm.

"Did you give her what she wanted?" she asked, trying to focus on what they'd been saying.

He stared down at her hand, as if waiting for her to remove it. She wondered why she didn't.

"Not entirely, but I told the attorneys to settle. What the hell did I care, anyway? I just wanted out." His eyes, dark pools in the shadowed car, raised to meet hers. "I wanted to come home."

June drowned in the look he was giving her. She drew away.

"You spent years trying to make your marriage work before you decided to divorce Kimberly," she pointed out. "You loved her."

He shook his head slowly. "No, I'd made a commitment. The Hardy men keep their commitments. The only time I didn't, the one time I didn't do what I knew was right was with–" he broke off.

Her. The one time he'd made a commitment and hadn't

kept it had been with her.

June turned to look out at her car, gleaming under the pickup's flashing lights. On...off. On...off.

Another vehicle, an SUV, came down the road and slowed when it reached them, but Calvin opened his window and waved it on. It picked up speed again, the headlights blinding for a moment as it moved passed, and was soon out of sight.

She felt like they were alone in the world, in the dark, in the cab of his truck while the hazard lights flashed.

"As soon as I left you, I knew it was wrong," he said quietly. She felt him watching her, but didn't meet his eyes. "I knew I'd made a mistake. The biggest mistake of my life. But I didn't know how to come back. I'd been so harsh when I left, I didn't know how to beg you to forgive me, how to grovel. Didn't know if you would even listen to me. Then I met Kimberly and figured I had to try and move on. I couldn't get back what I'd thrown away."

June was quiet for a moment, listening to the rumble of the pickup's engine.

"I would have listened," she said finally. "But," she added, because the moment called for honesty, "you'd have had to work pretty hard at it. I was...hurt."

Talk about an understatement. The wound had been so deep, so vast, even breathing caused pain.

He'd asked her to meet him at their favorite place, a park near the waterfall that gave the town its name. She'd thought he'd make love to her in the grass, in a secluded spot they'd discovered by accident and used often. She'd hoped he might say the three little words she'd been dying to hear from him.

But he hadn't told her he loved her. Instead, he'd told her that he'd been thinking about it, and he didn't want to see her anymore.

After all, he had graduated college with his master's degree, had trained to be an architect, and he'd just gotten an offer from a big firm in Philadelphia. He'd only been in Hardy Falls over the summer to take a break before he got on with the rest of his life. And she was a waitress at the local bar. It obviously wasn't going to work out between them, so they should break things off sooner rather than later.

He hadn't been angry or intentionally mean as he'd sliced her up and ripped out her heart. He'd been kind, logical. And he'd told her that he'd miss her, thanked her for a wonderful summer, and wished her all the best. He'd kissed her on the brow and left.

She'd stood there staring at the Hardy Falls waterfall. Twenty-three years old, feeling like ninety. Then her legs had given out, and she'd knelt in the long grass, in the mud left by a recent storm, and covered her face with her hands.

A week later, she heard he'd left town for that firm in Philadelphia. The next year, she found out he'd married Kimberly and that his career was taking off.

But he'd never tried to contact her. She wondered what would have happened if he had?

"You went out of your way to avoid me when you came to town to see your parents," she said when she could talk again.

"You avoided me, too," he correctly pointed out, then sighed. "After I got married, I didn't want everyone to think I was just looking for something on the side. I knew there'd be talk if we were seen together. I'd already hurt you enough; I didn't want to put that on you, too."

"And now?" she asked, her voice feeling like sandpaper in her throat.

He trapped her in that dark gaze again. "Now I'm divorced," he said. "And I'm here for good."

Bright lights came up behind them, and June heard the thunder of a truck over the pounding of her heart.

"Richie's here," Calvin said and got out of the pickup.

After pulling some oxygen into her lungs, June did, too.

8

June stood out of the way while the Dunlop Garage tow truck came to a heavy, grinding stop next to her car. A moment later, Richie Dunlop jumped down to the road. His uniform of bib overalls and work boots made him appear bigger than he really was, but his face, with its close-set eyes and long, narrow nose, still reminded her of a rat.

Truth in advertising, she thought.

He walked to them, his beady, rodent eyes running over June like insects. She wanted to kick him in the balls.

Finally, he turned his attention to Calvin. "Cal."

"Richie," Calvin said. He had his feet firmly planted and his arms crossed over his chest. "We need you to tow June's car to Wally's garage."

"Yeah, that's what you said." Richie dug in the front pocket of his overalls and pulled out a pack of cigarettes. He lit one and took a deep drag.

"And will you do that?" Calvin asked gently.

June glanced at him. Unless things had radically changed over the years, that tone of voice did not bode well.

"Well, I *will*," Richie said, as he blew out smoke and grinned at June, "but I need cash in advance."

What the hell?

"That's bullshit!" June exploded. "Wally didn't charge Hannah anything upfront when her car broke down a few weeks ago. He just added the cost of towing to the repair bill."

"That was Hannah. We knew she was good for it." Richie shrugged, the rest of the sentence unspoken.

And you're not.

"Listen you—" June snarled, but Calvin stopped her by putting a hand on her arm.

"I'll guarantee the bill," he said.

June, thoroughly aggravated now, rounded on him.

"I don't need you to guarantee my bill. I can guarantee my own damned bill." She spun back to Richie. "How much?" she demanded.

Richie tucked his free hand into his overalls and blew out another stream of smoke. June wanted to stuff the cigarette down his throat. She'd quit a couple of years ago, but the smell of the tobacco on top of the stress of the day was putting her cravings into overdrive. She had a pack of gum, but it was in her purse in Calvin's pickup truck.

"Two fifty."

June forgot all about cigarette cravings.

"Two fifty?" she shook off Calvin's restraining hand and took a step toward Richie. "Are you fucking kidding me? The garage is, what, five miles away?"

Richie shrugged again. "Late at night. Don't look to me like you have much of a choice. Even if you had one of them fancy auto road service plans, I'm the towing for this area. I'll charge what I want." He smirked.

"I'll leave it here, then," June said. "It'll wait for Wally tomorrow."

Richie's smile broadened. "Sure about that? Mighty dark

out here. Lots can happen to a deserted car on the side of the road."

June clenched her fists.

"I think you might want to reconsider, Richie," Calvin said, still quiet.

The tow truck driver snorted derisively.

"Yeah? Why? Because you're the fucking prince of Hardy Falls? This is my tow truck, my business, and I can do whatever the hell I want."

"Not exactly," Calvin said.

Richie seemed suddenly wary. "What the hell does that mean?" he demanded.

Calvin tugged his ear. "Well, first I think I'll call the road service companies and tell them you're extorting money when you make towing calls for them."

"So what?" Richie scoffed. "Some out of towners complained once or twice. But there weren't no proof. Can't do a thing without proof, and the road service people don't want to lose us. In case you haven't noticed, there ain't no other towing company around here."

"Or, better yet, maybe you'd like a visit from an inspector?" Calvin mused. "Maybe Wally would enjoy having someone from the licensing board drop in to see him? That can be arranged if you don't treat June right." He smiled. "I know a lot of people."

Richie looked at June. She crossed her arms and glared back at him.

"One twenty-five," he said abruptly.

It took her a moment to realize he was saying he'd charge her one hundred and twenty-five dollars to tow her car.

June saw Calvin incline his head slightly.

"I'll get my purse," she said.

"No." Calvin spoke when she would have moved off.

"Richie's going to roll his charge into the cost of service, just like Wally did for Hannah. Right?" he asked the other man.

Richie chewed on the end of his cigarette until he had to spit it out because he'd bitten through the filter. He stomped out the small flame, then glowered at Calvin.

"Right." His voice sounded like he'd swallowed rust.

Calvin nodded. "Good."

"I need your keys," Richie told her. She pulled her key ring out of her pocket and detached the car key and fob, handing them over to him. Without a word, he snatched them from her and stomped off.

"Are you sure threatening Richie was a good idea?" June asked Calvin when the other man was out of earshot.

He shrugged. "If he tries something, I can make good on the threats. I really do have some contacts with state inspectors."

June studied him. "You do?"

"Sure. I was a project manager at the architectural firm I worked for in Philly. Then I was managing everything in my own business. I know people. I think I'd better go make sure he doesn't try to mess with your car."

June watched him walk over to the tow truck.

Calvin had given up a lot to come back home. She'd never really thought about that aspect of things before. He'd left a lucrative career, and was now running a hardware store teetering on the edge of bankruptcy. Because he'd stopped fighting the divorce, because he'd told his attorneys to settle, it sounded like his bitch of an ex-wife ended up with more than her fair share of things.

Why?

Because he'd wanted to come home.

June frowned, folded her arms tighter against her chest, and went to stand next to Calvin.

Richie had moved the tow truck up behind her sedan and lowered the truck's flatbed to an angle. He pulled some tow lines, hooked them up to the car, and walked back to the truck. There was a roar of machinery and the lines tightened, tugging her car up the angled slope. Once it was in position, the flatbed of the truck leveled, taking the car along with it.

Calvin smiled with satisfaction, the harsh light of the headlights emphasizing the creases around his eyes and mouth. It was still a surprise to see the marks of age on his face; she tended to forget that he wasn't the twenty-four-year-old kid she'd known.

If she could believe what he said, he'd stayed with his wife because he'd wanted to honor his commitment. So, why had he finally decided to ask for a divorce? What had changed?

Richie finished securing her car to the tow truck and came to face them.

"I'll leave it at Wally's," he told her abruptly. "I'll put your key in the drop, so call him tomorrow."

"The car had better be there, or I'll know who took it," Calvin warned.

Richie sneered at him. "You think I'm stupid? It'll be there."

The two men exchanged such a long look that June wanted to tell them to just whip out their dicks and compare. Then Richie grunted and went back to his truck without offering June a ride; not that she would have accepted one. The tow truck growled to life, and he drove away.

Calvin turned to June. "Let's go."

She nodded, and they climbed back into the pickup.

"I'll need your address," Calvin said as he buckled his seatbelt.

"Do you know where Ms. Gregory's house is?" she asked.

"Sure."

"I live in the apartment over her garage."

Calvin paused, one hand on the steering wheel, the other on the gear shift. "Really? I know that place. It's like, what, two hundred square feet?"

She frowned. So her apartment was small. The rent was cheap, and there was less to clean.

"Probably more like three hundred. What's it to you?"

"Huh." He put the truck in gear, flipped off the hazard lights, and pulled out onto the road. "Well, I can tell you the plumbing's good," he said. "I did it myself."

She stared at him. "You did? When?" It definitely hadn't been since she'd been living there, and she'd been renting from Ms. Gregory for over three years.

"A while ago. The place was vacant, so it must have been before you moved in."

"I didn't know you were a plumber." When had that happened?

"I'm really not, but I can do basic stuff, and it didn't need much. It had already passed inspection, so it just needed new fixtures and some tweaking. She'd had a contractor, but they didn't see eye to eye, so she'd fired the guy." Calvin shook his head. "Anyway, she was stuck, so I told her I'd help." He laughed. "She watched me like a hawk the whole time I was there. Ms. Gregory can be...particular. She wasn't taking any chances."

June smiled because "particular" was one way to describe her landlady. "Pain in the ass" was another. She couldn't fault her, though. Ms. Gregory just wanted things done a certain way. Because she was an older woman, people sometimes thought they could take advantage of her. She didn't let them. Nothing wrong with that.

"She's my hero," she told him. "I want to be just like her when I grow up."

"Great," he muttered.

June laughed. "It was nice of you to help her out."

Calvin shrugged.

After a few minutes of companionable silence, he turned the pickup into the gravel driveway that ran next to Ms. Gregory's neat white house and drove back to the two car garage behind it.

As they rumbled to a stop near the stairs leading to June's tiny apartment, it suddenly occurred to her that the sound of the truck's engine had probably woken Ms. Gregory, who would know June had not come home in her own car. And, since she suspected Albert Cromwell was in the house with her landlady, June would more than likely get questioned by both of them later.

Damned small towns.

"Couldn't own a regular car, could you?" she complained to Calvin as he shifted into park and she unhooked her seatbelt. "Had to have a monster truck."

He grinned. "Go big or go home."

"Yeah, yeah." She looked at him. "So, thanks for stopping and bailing me out."

"So, you're welcome."

Acting on impulse, June leaned over and kissed him on his lean cheek, right where the corner of his mouth had deepened with amusement.

She'd intended the gesture to be casual, friendly. Calvin had been good to her that night, and she wanted—maybe wanted—to get to know him again. To not carry around so much pain and resentment. Maybe they could, eventually, get to the point where they could talk without the past getting in the way.

But as she drew back, he reached up and clamped his hands on her arms, holding her in place. He stared down at her, his eyes dark in the dim light.

"June," he whispered. He wasn't hurting her, but she couldn't move either.

"Let go," she said. She'd wanted to sound firm, but the words came out as a choked gasp.

He shook his head slightly. "I never forgot you, June," he

said, his breath ghosting across her face. "You were always there with me."

"Except I wasn't. You were gone, and I was here." She tried not to feel anything, tried to ignore the way the heat of his body surrounded her in the close confines of the truck. It was impossible.

"I'm so sorry I hurt you," he murmured. "So sorry."

"That's guilt," she told him, a little desperately. "You don't even know me anymore. You're remembering a girl who hasn't been around for a long time."

"No."

She didn't even see the kiss coming. One moment she was staring into his face, the next his mouth was on hers, taking possession of it. The taste of him, of Calvin, roared through her like a freight train. It was familiar, yet different; like a food you knew you'd been craving, but hadn't been able to indulge in for a long, long time.

Her lips parted involuntarily when he demanded entry, and his flavor exploded across her tongue. He plundered her mouth the way he used to do, as if she was the sole focus of his world, his only thought and consideration.

She should have shoved him back, but she was so damned hungry for him. All these years and nobody had ever measured up to the memory of him. To taste him again, smell him, touch him, made her crazy. She broke away to breathe and realized she'd wrapped her arms around his neck, pressed her breasts against his chest, dug her fingers into his hair.

"June." He kissed her again and tugged her camp shirt out of her jeans. Then his hands—those clever, clever hands—were on her skin, setting her on fire. He cupped a breast, tweaked the nipple through her bra, and she moaned into his mouth. Without quite knowing how she'd gotten there, she was suddenly on his lap with her shirt open to the waist. He was busily trying to unhook her bra, but since he wouldn't stop kissing her, he wasn't having much luck.

Sucking his tongue into her mouth, she let go of his hair with one of her hands and ran it down his hard, muscled chest until she could rub the impressive erection she was straddling. She squeezed it, and Calvin jerked in response, which pressed her up against the steering wheel.

The loud blast of the truck's horn cut through June's passion like a knife through butter, snapping her back to her senses.

What the hell was she doing?

She pushed at Calvin, and he let her go. Buttoning her shirt with shaking fingers, she retreated quickly to her own seat.

"What...?" she gasped. "What are you trying to prove?" It maddened her to realize that all she wanted was to taste him again. She scrambled for the door handle, desperate to get out of the truck before she did something even more stupid than what she'd already done.

"Sorry," he panted, breathless.

"Right."

"Go out to dinner with me."

She stared at him incredulously. "You have got to be kidding me."

"No." His hair was mussed, his lips were swollen from their kiss, and his shirt was as rumpled as her own. "I want to see you again, June."

She was pretty sure *seeing her* wasn't all he wanted to do.

"Go to hell." She finally managed to get the door open and jumped out before slamming it closed in his face. Then she all but ran for the stairs, climbing them quickly, needing to get away from him.

Calvin, being Calvin, didn't just drive off. No, he sat there in his noisy truck while she fumbled the key out of her purse and opened the door. He waited for her to turn on a light inside the apartment before finally backing up and driving off. Just like he was returning her home after a date.

June watched him go. Then she stepped back into the apartment, closed the door, and slumped against it.

Jesus.

Her heart was still pounding, and her lips were tingling. She could feel tenderness in various places where the shadow of his whiskers had scraped across her skin.

She drew in a deep breath.

He wanted her. No doubt he'd be more than happy to pick up where they'd left off.

What bothered her the most was that, at the moment, it seemed like a pretty good idea.

She pushed off the door and went to change. And to take a cold shower.

9

onsidering he hadn't gotten home until almost four o'clock in the morning, Calvin was in a damned good mood when he hauled himself out of bed after a measly couple hours of sleep and headed back into town to open the store. The reason was simple.

June.

God, holding her again, tasting her mouth, feeling her luscious body moving against his. She'd scorched him right down to the bone.

He drew in a deep breath through his nose.

Not now, he told himself. He couldn't think about kissing June anymore, or he'd end up with a hard-on as impressive as the one he'd sported the night before. Not a good idea when you were trying to appear at least semi-professional

True, she'd run like a rabbit when he'd asked her to dinner. But that thought only had him whistling a happy tune, while he navigated his pickup truck through the Hardy Falls version of early morning traffic.

June was definitely *not* indifferent.

He pulled Big Red into a parking spot behind Hardy Hardware and got out, yawning and stretching out his back before grabbing his to-go mug of hot, black coffee. He might be in a good mood, but caffeine was going to be essential today. He wasn't as young as he used to be.

Calvin walked to the building, jingled his keys around until he found the right one, and let himself into the store that had been part of his life for as long as he could remember. Yes, it would have been nice to stay in bed a while, but business was business. They had enough problems without pissing off customers by not keeping to their posted hours.

His father had offered to come in his place, but Calvin had told him that, since he'd slept longer and was more alert, he should stay home to handle Eva's morning routine until the health aide got there. His mother tended to forget what she was supposed to do, sometimes in the middle of doing it, with occasionally disastrous results. Constant supervision was necessary.

He took a slug of his coffee and flicked a switch to turn on some of the overhead fluorescent lighting. Then he powered up both registers, got cash out of the safe, stocked the drawers, and took care of the million tasks that needed to be done before Hardy Hardware and Building Supply opened for another day. They'd gotten their regular delivery from one of the wholesalers the day before, so, once things were basically under control, he carried boxes out into the showroom and slit them open to restock the shelves.

He smiled as he pulled out a bundle of boxes of roofing nails, remembering how much he'd hated stocking shelves when he was younger. All of the other kids had been out playing ball or doing whatever after school, but he'd often been stuck here, putting stuff on shelves or, if his father had decided to reorganize, moving it to other shelves. Sometimes he'd put things on the wrong shelves, just to see how long it took someone to notice. He'd been such a jackass.

The smile faded.

Yes, he'd been an ass. An arrogant, self-centered prick.

June might not be indifferent to him, she might have responded when he'd kissed her instead of slapping him across the face like he deserved, but that didn't mean she'd give him another chance.

The back door opened and Austin Grant, the sales associate scheduled to work that morning, strolled in. He was a tall, lanky kid with a thick thatch of blond hair and a bright, cocky grin useful for charming contractors. He was also studying to be a construction engineer at the local university, so he was a real asset to the store. Calvin reminded himself to talk to his father about giving the boy more responsibility.

"Hey, Mr. H. the Younger," Austin called. He shrugged out of his jacket, revealing his black uniform shirt with the interlocking "Hs" of the Hardy Hardware logo on its pocket.

"Hey, Austin," Calvin called in response. He pulled the polywrap off the boxes of roofing nails and started stacking them on the appropriate shelf. These days, everything went where it was supposed to go.

Austin ducked into the office to hang up his jacket, then walked up the aisle to stand next to Calvin.

"So, you have a good night?" he asked with a sly smile and studied casualness.

Calvin stopped stacking to consider him. "Yes," he said slowly. "Why?"

Austin pulled a hex nut out of a nearby bin and spun it on one of the shelves. "No reason," he said, still utterly casual. "But, um, I saw your pickup on the side of the road late last night. Well, early this morning. There was a sedan there, too. Everything okay?"

Great, Calvin thought. Austin must have been in the SUV that had driven past after Bernie had gone.

"Everything's fine," he said.

Austin's grin widened, and he dropped the nut back into the

bin with the others. "See, I knew that truck was Big Red. Who else owns a bright red monster pickup truck around here? My buddies and I saw the flashing lights when we were heading home and thought we'd stop to see what was up. You waved us on, so we kept going." He smirked. "But when we went past, our headlights kind of lit up the cab. Looked like two people sitting inside."

"That was June Esperanza," Calvin said. "We were waiting for Richie Dunlop to get there with his tow truck." No sense denying anything since Bernie and Richie were sure to share what they'd seen. Besides, it wasn't like he was ashamed to be caught with June. In fact, he was kind of proud.

"Thought so." Austin rocked back on the heels of his work boots and shoved his hands into his pockets. "The guy who was driving—Mike—works at Dunlop Garage, and he said he was sure the sedan belonged to her. He works on it a lot." Austin knocked Calvin on the shoulder. "Good job, boss man. She is smoking hot."

"She broke down. I was helping her out."

"Sure, sure." The kid flashed another cheeky grin. "But you *do* look a little tired this morning."

Calvin tamped down a sudden flare of protective anger at the insinuation.

"June is a friend of mine," he said coldly. "I helped her last night because I found her broken down on the side of the road. I look tired today because I didn't get home until after three thirty in the morning. End of story."

Austin's grin faded.

"Um, okay," he said. "Sorry. Just kidding around, man. I didn't mean anything."

"I know," Calvin forced a tight smile, "but I wanted to set the record straight. Wouldn't want there to be a lot of hearsay going around about June."

Austin shrugged. "We were mostly talking about you," he

said guilelessly. "You haven't picked up a woman since you've been back in town. Haven't even looked at one, as far as anyone can tell. Women come on to you plenty, but you just ignore them."

"I've been busy!" Calvin defended himself.

"Yeah, well, whatever. My parents said you dated June back in the day, so they figured you might be starting up with her again. My dad, he said he wouldn't be surprised, considering how hot and heavy you two used to be."

Calvin blinked. "You've already talked to your parents about this?"

"Well, sure." Austin seemed surprised. "At breakfast. I kind of live with them, you know?"

"I know." Calvin rubbed his hands through his hair. He'd forgotten Austin lived at home, not in the dorms at school. He also needed this conversation to be over before he found out what else the Grant family had said about him.

"Look," he said, pulling out his business-owner voice, "why don't you finish stocking the shelves while I go check the special orders. Joe Horton's been bugging me for his stuff, so he'll probably be in as soon as we open."

"Sure," Austin said with his usual cheer. "I'm on it." He bent down and began to sort through the boxes on the floor.

Calvin left him to it, grabbed his coffee mug, and went to the storage room, where they put the special orders.

Rolling his shoulders to shake off any lingering irritation, he gulped another lifesaving hit of coffee, put the mug on an old desk jammed into a corner of the crowded space, then rifled through a neat stack of forms in a wire rack. He pulled out Joe Horton's order and took it over to the boxes he had stowed the day before. If Joe's shipment wasn't right, he wanted to know about it before the old man came in. Hardy Hardware made it a policy to treat their good customers like royalty; it was the only way they had a prayer of competing with the chain store in the next town.

Calvin opened the first box and started sorting and checking the contents against the order form.

Austin had called June smoking hot. Well, he'd been right about that much.

He frowned, put the first box aside and opened the second. This one was full of different sized fan belts, and he pulled out packages to check them against the paperwork.

He'd expected there would be talk, but it was still unsettling to think of Austin and his parents speculating about him over the breakfast table. He guessed he'd gotten used to living in Center City. When you were in Philadelphia, nobody cared what the hell you did. You were just one more jerk on the subway. If you weren't going around murdering people, who even saw you? In Hardy Falls, your life was basically the town's entertainment.

He shifted his shoulders and put the second box in Joe's order on top of the first. Then he straightened, grabbed his mug, and walked over to a dusty window, finishing the coffee as he stared out at Big Red waiting patiently in the parking lot.

When he'd come under this kind of scrutiny before, he'd been twenty-four. Seeing June. He'd dealt with it by leaving.

Well, leaving wasn't an option this time, even if he wanted to. And the only way the rumors would die down was if he made it clear he'd only been helping June. If he stayed away from her.

Fuck that.

Calvin put the empty mug on the desk and turned back to Joe's order. He hefted up the two boxes and moved them closer to the door, where they would be easily accessible when the old man got there.

In fact, he thought, moving automatically to put the room back in order, maybe it would be a good idea to show everyone where he stood, June included. Maybe he needed to put himself out there so nobody would have any doubts.

He walked to the window, looked out at Big Red again.

She didn't trust him, and he sure couldn't blame her. He'd been so arrogant, such a young prick. Throwing away the best thing he'd ever had in his life.

If he really wanted June to give him a second chance, he was going to have to work for it. Make it completely obvious to her and everyone else that she was worth the effort.

Go big or go home.

He frowned, thinking.

He'd planned to call her later at the Country Time, or maybe see if someone would give him her cell phone number. He wanted to find out if she'd heard about her car, and ask her out on a date again. But that would be the safe, easy way to handle things, and she'd probably be expecting it. She'd assume he'd want to be discreet.

She thought she knew him, and he had to prove to her that she didn't.

A plan of action started to form in his mind, and he smiled out at Big Red.

Screw discretion. Hardy Falls could just bring it on.

Still smiling, he turned and got back to work.

About the time Joe Horton, Albert Cromwell, Martin Scanner, and Harry Newman descended on Hardy Hardware and began grilling Calvin about gossip they'd heard that morning at the diner, and how Albert had seen a pickup truck at June's apartment, June herself finally gave up trying to sleep.

Whenever she closed her eyes, her stupid mind insisted on thinking about Calvin, remembering his kiss, the way he tasted, the warmth of his hard body wrapped around hers. The few times she'd actually managed to drift off, she'd dreamed about him and jerked awake feeling aroused, itchy, and unsatisfied.

So, even though it was way too freaking early for her to be up, she dragged herself out of bed and into the shower. Still pissed off at the world in general, she made a pot of brutally strong coffee and drank the first cup while glaring out her kitchen/living room window at the squirrels frolicking in Ms. Gregory's tidy backyard.

A particularly chubby squirrel started climbing the pole to a round bird feeder set a respectful distance from the flower garden. When it was halfway up the pole, it launched itself onto the feeder, then held on for dear life as the feeder's base began spinning, set in motion by the weight of the intruder. A moment later the chubby squirrel went flying and landed face-first on a patch of grass.

Ms. Gregory's new, hideously expensive, squirrel-proof feeder had claimed its latest victim.

"That's the story of my life, buddy," June told the squirrel, watching it shake off the fall and groom its fur into order. It ran back to the feeder pole and started climbing again, a determined glint in its beady eyes.

Maybe that was the story of her life, too.

June put down her coffee mug, turned away from the window, and called Wallace Dunlop.

The garage owner had looked at her car personally, but when she heard his report, June kind of wished he hadn't taken the time. Her alternator, he told her, was deader than disco, her battery was shot, and, as a bonus, he'd found a leak in the power steering system.

June thanked him, hung up, and called Claude Beecher. After being transferred four different times, and put on hold for at least fifteen minutes, she told the receptionist, very kindly, that she would be coming in to deliver her message personally unless she spoke to Claude right away. He was on the phone a minute later, making disgusting cooing noises. Oh no, she'd broken down, again? Wasn't that just too bad?

"I want you to reimburse me for the cost of replacing the alternator," she said, interrupting him mid-coo.

"Now, June," he soothed, "you know I can't do that."

"I'll sue," she threatened.

"You certainly have the right. I don't even blame you for trying," he said, good-naturedly. "But you know, court cases can get mighty expensive, and you probably won't win."

"What about the lemon law?" she challenged.

"Used car," he pointed out. "Not covered in Pennsylvania."

"The warranty—"

"Specifically states that it doesn't cover normal and expected repairs," Claude said, voice filled with regret. "Everything that's gone wrong up to this point falls into that category. And you purchased a basic warranty, so the electrical system's not covered either. I'm sorry you're not happy, but—"

She hung up on him.

Then she dialed Hannah.

"I need a ride to work," she snapped as soon as the younger woman picked up.

"Okay." Hannah yawned, a long, drawn out sound, and June realized she'd probably been asleep. Too freaking bad. "Mind telling me why?"

"Because my goddamned car died on the side of the road last night, that's why."

"What?" Hannah sounded instantly more alert. "Are you okay? Why didn't you call me?"

"I'm fine," June said, calming down a bit at the other woman's evident concern. "Calvin helped me."

Hannah was silent for a moment.

"Calvin?" she asked hesitantly. "Calvin Hardy?"

"Do you know any other Calvins in this godforsaken town?" June demanded. "Of course Calvin Hardy."

"I didn't—"

"Can you give me a ride to work or not?" she interrupted.

"Sure," Hannah said hastily. "I have to go in early today, so I'll be at your place around noon. Will that be okay?"

"I'll bring a book. Thanks." June hung up. She stood, breathing through her teeth, watching squirrels get thrown off the bird feeder. They seemed to be lining up to take turns.

"It's all fun and games until someone kicks you in the nuts," she told them.

Drawing her hands through her hair, she sighed and started pacing around her tiny apartment.

If she didn't pay to fix the car's alternator, she wouldn't be able to sell it for enough money to pay off the loan she'd taken out to buy the thing. If she paid to fix it and sold the car, she might be able to pay off the existing loan, but she'd definitely need a new loan to buy a different car. Either way, her savings would be gone.

In other words, she was screwed.

June cursed. She should probably just give in and get a second job, but *hell*, it galled her to think this mistake of a car was going to force her to go there. She loved having time on her days off to wander around town or in the woods, taking pictures of whatever struck her fancy. Until she'd started getting into photography, she hadn't fully appreciated the beauty of the area.

Her photos were even getting kind of good, in spite of the fact that she only had a cheap point-and-shoot digital camera. If she could upgrade the camera and get better at the editing program Mary Alice had installed on her computer, she might be able to take things to the next level. There wouldn't be a lot of time to do that if she had to work two jobs.

Maybe she could combine her interests? Pick up some extra money taking wedding photos? Or pictures of kids?

June laughed out loud at the thought of her working as a

wedding photographer or at some kid's party. No freaking way. People usually wanted to live through their special occasion, not get hit over the head with a camera before it was finished.

The phone rang, interrupting her thoughts, and she grabbed for it without checking the caller ID.

"Yes," she said, expecting it to be Wally or maybe Hannah.

"June."

Pat Murphy.

June rolled her eyes to the ceiling. Really? *Really*?

"Pat. What's up?"

"Heard you broke down last night. Everything okay?"

"Well, it sure doesn't take long for news to get around, does it? Did Bernie tell you? Or was it Claude? Or maybe Richie?"

"Of course it was Bernie. Bastard couldn't wait to let me know he'd come across you and Calvin Hardy all snuggled up tight waiting for a tow." Pat sounded bitter. "I thought it was just a story at first, but Wally said your car really is in the garage."

"Checking up on me, Pat?" she asked softly.

"Just a conversation at the diner this morning. So, are you all right or what?"

"I'm fine."

"Why didn't you call me?"

"Why would I call you?" she countered, ignoring for the moment that she couldn't have called anyone since her phone had been dead. If she had been able to call someone, it sure as hell wouldn't have been Pat.

"Right. Why would you?" His voice was harsh. "Especially since you had Hardy right where you wanted him. Fucking convenient, wasn't it? Up to your old tricks, June?"

She closed her eyes. "Pat. Listen. I'm sorry I hurt you, but we're over. Let it go."

"Sure." He hung up.

"Wonderful." June tossed the phone on a table and wandered back to the window, wrapping her arms around her suddenly chilled body. She stared sightlessly out at the lush woods beyond Ms. Gregory's gardens, past the bird feeder with the flying squirrels.

She wasn't surprised rumors had already started, not with Bernie and Richie involved. And she wasn't shocked at all that Bernie had gone right to Pat; the asshole just loved getting people stirred up.

The whole town would be buzzing. Not only had June been caught with a man on the side of the road in the middle of the night, but that man had been—gasp!—Calvin Hardy. And if Ms. Gregory or Albert mentioned hearing the truck and the horn? Signed, sealed, and delivered. Hell, with her luck, Ms. Gregory would put an article in her online newspaper.

Nothing new, June reminded herself. She was certainly used to being the subject of talk in Hardy Falls. She'd never cared what people thought about her, but she'd often wondered if the gossip floating around fifteen years ago had been the real reason Calvin had dumped her.

It had been pretty bad then, with lots of people thinking she was a party girl at best or a whore at worst. There'd also been speculation about drug use, and for a while the police chief at the time had come to check on her whereabouts whenever something went missing.

Had Calvin believed what people said about her?

Did he still believe it?

She frowned.

Why did it suddenly matter what Calvin believed?

June started pacing, this time because a dull, low-level craving for a cigarette had flared up. Swear to God, she'd craved cigarettes more in the past two months than she had in all of the last two years.

Would Calvin call? Check to see how she was? Push the whole "date" thing? He'd said he wanted to see her again.

No, probably not, she decided. First of all, he didn't have her phone numbers, although he could certainly track her down if he wanted to. But it was likely word had already gotten back to him about them being the topic of conversation in town. If he didn't know already, he definitely would soon. Which meant she probably wouldn't hear from Calvin again.

She just wished that thought made her happier.

10

—————

True to her word, Hannah picked June up promptly at noon. A few minutes later, they were buzzing down the highway in the younger woman's compact car.

"I'm sorry you're going to be so early," Hannah said, her attention on the road as she guided the car through a curve. "I have a meeting today with Uncle George to review the books."

Hannah's uncle was the accountant for the Country Time and had been for a few years now. June wouldn't have trusted the man as far as she could throw him, but Hannah seemed satisfied.

"No big deal. I'm just glad you could give me a lift, so I didn't have to make Mary Alice or Deacon come out of their way to get me." June tried to stretch her legs, with limited success.

Hannah frowned. "I wish we could force Claude to give you some of your money back. That car's been nothing but trouble."

"Tell me about it," June grimaced. "But the bastard's right when he says the warranty doesn't cover the things that have gone wrong."

They drove without speaking for a few moments, the only sound the hum of tires on asphalt.

"You really can't kill him," Hannah said at last.

"Yeah, then I'd never get any money out of him."

Hannah glanced at her. "It worries me *that's* the only reason you can come up with for not committing murder."

June shrugged.

When they got to the Country Time, Hannah hurried to her office, and June went to the kitchen locker for an apron. She'd brought a book but had too much nervous energy to sit and read. So she'd clean instead. There was always something that needed cleaning at the Country Time.

After pulling on thick, yellow rubber gloves, she tackled the grill. Working methodically, the smell of the cleanser strong in her nostrils, she scoured until the old stainless steel shone like new, then turned to give the prep counters the same treatment.

She'd charged her goddamned cell phone, and actually had it in her pocket, but nobody had called. June scrubbed harder when she realized she still thought she might hear from Calvin.

Stupid. So stupid.

She stopped scouring and straightened, a little winded.

One night, one meeting, one kiss, and here she was, getting sucked back into the fantasy.

Hannah came strolling into the kitchen and goggled at the gleaming grill.

"Jeez, June. You weren't supposed to be working yet."

June scowled at her, stripped off her gloves, and threw them towards the sink. "I was bored. What are you doing here?"

Hannah blinked at her. "Um, we're opening soon, so I was going to get ready." She looked around. "Although it seems like you already did most of it."

"I'll take care of things until Kevin gets here," June told her. She needed to keep busy.

"You will?" Hannah asked suspiciously.

"Yeah. Get the hell out of my kitchen."

Hannah got the hell out.

Deacon came in through the back door a few minutes later. He raised his eyebrows when he saw the sparkling kitchen but wisely made no comment. Instead, he waved a greeting and headed to the bar to begin his own preparations. Deacon always did have common sense.

People started trickling in as soon as they opened: the early drinkers and the people coming in for food and beer after their shifts ended. Hannah or Deacon brought June food orders, and soon she had burgers, dogs, and wings going. The familiar scent of grilled meat overrode the smell of bleach, calming her.

Kevin came in sometime before five for his shift, staring when he saw the state of the kitchen, even though the effect was diminished since she'd been working for a while.

"You cleaned," he said.

June turned away from the grill and fisted her hands on her hips to glare at him. "Yes. I freaking cleaned. Want to make something of it?"

He held up his big, ham-sized hands and took a step back. "*Non.* I am grateful, no?"

"You should be."

He looked around the kitchen again and shook his head. "You clean the fryer, too?" he asked hopefully. "I hate that bitch."

"Hell, no. Would I steal all your fun?"

"June—" Hannah pushed through the kitchen door. "Oh, hi, Kevin."

"Boss lady." He grinned at her as he headed to get an apron.

"I know it's early, but we're getting busy," Hannah told June. "Since you're here, would you mind if we started table service? Mary Alice should be in soon, anyway, and..." she broke off, looking stricken. "Oh, crap. No. Forget I said anything. I'll do it."

"Why?" June demanded, although she had an idea. "It's my job, isn't it?"

Hannah glanced back towards the taproom. "Bernie and Chet are already out there. Bernie's telling everyone about how he found you and Calvin on the side of the road."

Of course he was.

"Then I guess I'd better go show my face, huh? Don't want that asshole to think I'm afraid of him."

"June—" Hannah gnawed on her bottom lip. "I wasn't thinking...I didn't mean..."

"Hannah." June put her hands on the other woman's arms. "I'm not going to hide here in the kitchen. I know I did last night, but I was a coward, and it won't happen again. I live in this goddamned town, and I'm gonna do my job," she bared her teeth, "with a freaking smile."

Hannah gulped. "Okay." Now she looked worried for a different reason. "You won't hurt Bernie, will you?"

"Is he sitting at the bar?"

Hannah nodded.

"Then I won't even talk to him," June promised. She stripped off her greasy apron and threw it towards the laundry tub, then untied her hair and shook it out. "But if Claude Beecher shows up, all bets are off."

She turned and pushed through the kitchen door as Hannah quickly pulled out her cell phone and dialed. The girl was probably going to warn Claude to stay away tonight, which was just a damned shame.

June paused at the end of the bar to collect an order pad and pencil and saw Hannah had been right. The place was really filling up, even though it was early. Well, that wasn't too unusual for a Friday night. There just wasn't a heck of a lot else to do in Hardy Falls. Add in some juicy gossip, and the whole town would probably turn out.

Bernie and Chet were watching her avidly from their seats

at the other end of the bar, but Deacon had things under control, so June ignored the dynamic duo and headed out to the tables and booths. Through sheer force of will, she plastered on a smile, refused to acknowledge the stares, took orders, joked with the regulars, and basically fell into her normal routine of relatively jovial server. What she'd told Hannah was true; she lived in this town, so she might as well meet this latest drama head-on.

"Hey, Junebug," Harry Newman said when she brought him a draft beer, his smile sweet in his lined and weathered garden-gnome face. Even though he was the only one of Old Albert's cronies who was married, he still managed to spend almost every night at the Country Time. Apparently, his wife preferred it that way.

"Hey, Harry," she returned, leaning her hip companionably against his table. "Where are all of your friends?"

"I expect they'll be along." Harry took a pull of his beer and put the glass back on the table. "What's all this I hear about you making out with Calvin Hardy on the side of the road last night?"

June rolled her eyes, although her stomach clenched. "Who fed you that bullshit? I bet it was Bernie Housemann."

Harry watched her with brown eyes that had seen more than their fair share of life. "Bernie, Richie, Pat, Milo."

"Who's Milo?" June asked, distracted. "The name's familiar, but I can't place him."

"Milo Grant. On a bowling league, lives out on Mulvaney Street. You know him—he's the one who insists on wearing that damned Mets baseball hat."

"Oh, him." Now June could picture a stocky, blond man who wore his Mets colors with pride. Had to give the guy credit for having balls; there weren't many who would be brave enough to walk into the Country Time dressed like that. Especially if the Mets had made post-season play and the

Phillies were out of it. Fortunately, both teams were usually out of it.

"Why does he care what I was doing last night?" she asked.

"Everyone in town cares," Harry pointed out. "Milo said his kid and some friends were out driving around last night and saw a pickup and a sedan parked on the side of the road. They tried to stop, but were waved off."

"Oh." Must have been the SUV.

"Apparently one of the friends recognized your sedan, and Milo's kid knew Calvin's truck because he works at the hardware store."

Terrific.

"Look," she told Harry. "My alternator died. Calvin and I were just waiting for the tow truck to get there."

"Uh huh." Harry took another sip of beer. "So why did Albert hear a pickup truck drive up Mathilda Gregory's driveway, idle in front of your apartment for several minutes, blow its horn unexpectedly, idle a few more minutes, and drive away at approximately three thirty this morning?"

June stared at him. "What the hell did he do? File a police report? I thought he and Ms. Gregory were busy."

Harry shrugged. "Man pays attention to details."

"Oh, for...!" June threw her free hand wide. "Calvin drove me home. We talked. That's all there is to it."

"Of course it is," Harry soothed.

"And everyone in this town can just mind their own freaking business for once in their damned lives."

Harry patted her arm, smiled at her as if she was delusional, and ordered a burger.

June stomped off to place his order. When she returned with the food, Albert, Joe, and Martin were all at the table, too.

"Stop!" she said, raising a hand to fend them off as she put down Harry's plate. "Nothing happened. Calvin helped me. My alternator died. Richie towed the car to Wally's shop. Calvin took me home. We talked. Claude Beecher is a butt-bag. That is all." She held up her order pad. "What can I get you?"

"Why did the truck horn go off when you were parked in front of your apartment?" Albert waggled bushy eyebrows. "I know why horns go off when I'm with a woman in *my* truck. Not a lot of room in those cabs."

"You told us angels sing when you're with a woman in your truck," Joe said.

"That's because Albert usually needs some divine intervention," Martin told him.

"Not since that there pill came along. That's God in a prescription, boys." Albert grinned toothlessly, as his friends laughed. "I mean," he continued, turning back to June, "in my experience, when a horn goes off like that, there's usually some canoodling happening there on the front seat."

June raised her eyebrows. "Canoodling?"

"Canoodling."

She thought about why that horn had gone off and gave Albert the black stare of death. "Do you want me to take your freaking order or not?" she demanded.

He grinned, showing off his gums. "Yup," he said with some satisfaction and ordered hot wings. Joe and Martin followed suit. Harry asked for another burger.

June took the orders to the kitchen, ignoring Bernie's attempt to get her attention as she walked past. Mary Alice breezed in, looking like a wide-eyed dandelion with her flyaway hair pulled back in a bright yellow ribbon, and June made sure the other woman handled the section closest to Bernie and Chet.

After carrying plates of steaming, spicy wings and Harry's second hamburger back to the old men, she worked the room. She did her job, took food and drink orders, cleaned up spills, and pretended not to see the sideways looks or hear the snide remarks. Some people asked her outright what had happened the night before. If she liked the person, she answered. If she didn't, she smiled and walked away.

But, despite June's best efforts, her mood deteriorated, and her patience wore thin as time went on and the place got busier, the attention more intense.

Swear to God, for a bunch of hard-working, theoretically adult people, the citizens of Hardy Falls sure spent a lot of time wondering whether or not Calvin had actually gotten into her apartment, June thought. Of course, they were actually wondering whether or not he'd gotten into her pants.

When she practically threw a hotdog at Margo Truelove, who kept placing food orders so she could, with the subtlety of a blind elephant, question June about where Calvin had spent the night, Deacon came out from behind the bar, took her shoulders in his hands and steered her towards the kitchen.

"Break," he said. "Now."

"Fine," June snarled at him, more than willing to leave these assholes behind for a few minutes. She could see Bernie and Chet eavesdropping with ill-concealed interest, and almost made a leap for them, ready to plow her fist right into Bernie's blathering mouth. He'd be drinking his meals through a straw by the time she was done with him.

Deacon must have sensed her intentions because he all but shoved her through the kitchen door. Hannah and Kevin, both busy plating food orders, looked up in surprise.

"I'm taking a freaking break," she growled.

Hannah shrugged. "Okay."

June marched out the back door and collapsed into one of the plastic Adirondack lawn chairs behind the Country Time. She crossed her arms over her chest and glared at the trees on the other side of the parking lot.

Goddamned people. Goddamned town. Why was she still here again?

She drew in a deep breath and let it out.

Okay, so maybe she wasn't quite as used to being the subject of gossip as she'd thought she was. It was freaking irritating to have everyone speculating about you when you hadn't even done anything to deserve it. Who could blame Calvin for backing off?

Well, she could. And she did.

Although, didn't she want Calvin to back off? Didn't she want him to stay out of her life?

She did.

Her scowl intensified.

But really, he'd asked her out, kissed her, and then didn't even bother to find out if she'd made it to work okay without a car? Freaking typical. What had she expected?

June leaned her head back against the plastic chair.

Maybe, she thought, she should be more concerned about the fact she had been sort of assuming he would call, than worrying about the reason why he hadn't.

She was *such* an idiot.

Sighing, June pushed herself up and headed back inside. She'd get through the rest of the evening. Then tomorrow she'd do...whatever came next.

Hannah and Kevin watched her stalk through the kitchen, but neither one said anything. June didn't stop. If she tried to explain what was going on, Hannah would feel guilty and insist on taking her place out on the floor. June didn't want that, so she kept walking.

When she stepped out into the taproom, she spotted Mary Alice standing still in the sea of people, scribbling busily in her notepad. She might have even been taking an order, but the frowns on the faces of the people sitting closest to her said she was probably writing poetry or some shit.

June rolled her eyes and headed toward the other woman, intending to remind her where she was.

"June."

She pulled up short at the sound of the deep masculine voice calling her name and turned.

Calvin.

He was sitting at the bar, one foot hooked on the bar stool. Just like that, time seemed to vanish. Just like that, she wanted him again.

Which royally pissed her off.

"What are you doing here?" she demanded.

He smiled at her and held up a beer. "Drinking."

Now she felt stupid.

"Fine," she snapped.

"And maybe I wanted to see you."

She glowered at him. "Why?"

For a moment he seemed disconcerted. "What do you mean, 'Why?' I wanted to find out about your car. And I told you last night that I wanted to see you again."

She crossed her arms. "The car's under control. And I can't help but notice that you didn't even bother to call to find out if I'd made it into work today."

Calvin ran a hand through his hair, and it comforted her to know he was not as calm as he appeared. "I don't have your phone number."

"You could have found it. Or called here."

"I know, I know." He glanced around, then stood, straightening his shoulders. "June, I'm here to ask if you want to go out on a date. With me," he added.

There was an audible gasp from the people nearby.

June looked away from Calvin and realized they had the undivided attention of every person in the taproom. Country music still pounded over the loudspeakers, but the noise of talking and laughing had stopped, and the fine folks of Hardy Falls were staring at them with mute fascination. Even Deacon was watching from behind the bar, although he was probably just waiting to see if she needed help.

"Let's go outside," she told Calvin.

"No." He smiled down at her, reached out, and touched her cheek with his forefinger before letting his hand drop again. "So, will you? Go out with me? We could go to dinner. Maybe a movie."

What the hell was he trying to prove?

"Outside," she snapped.

Without pausing to see if he would follow, she shoved through the kitchen door, strode past Hannah and Kevin, and went out the back. This time, she didn't stop at the break area but walked all the way across the parking lot to the scrub trees lining the unplowed field beyond. She whirled around and took an involuntary step back when she realized Calvin was close on her heels. Recovering, she glared at him.

"What do you think you're doing?" she demanded.

Calvin studied her for a moment, his face shadowed in the dim light of the parking lot.

"I thought I was asking you out on a date," he said at last.

"In front of the whole town."

He thought about it, and nodded. "Yes."

She clasped her hands into fists and laughed without humor.

"Are you just trying to humiliate me?"

Calvin shook his head, baffled. "Humiliate you?" he growled. "How the hell are you being humiliated? I'm the one who's putting himself out there to show you I'm willing to take a chance. Just freaking say 'no' if you don't want to go."

"You asked in front of everyone." June set her teeth when her chin wanted to wobble. "They already act like we're their own damned reality television show. Now they're going to be watching us even more closely."

He took a step toward her, crowding her back against a tree. "I want to see you, and I'm not ashamed of that. I'm not going to hide, not now. I'm not going to back away unless you tell me to. Fuck everyone else."

She stared up into his hard face, wondering if she could believe what he was saying.

"You do realize that if I turn you down, they'll be talking about me, not you," she pointed out.

"Bullshit."

"They will. I can hear them now." She deepened her voice into a fair imitation of Bernie. "June Esperanza turned down Calvin Hardy? Who does she think she is? Ain't like she's gonna get a better offer in this town. Nah, Calvin probably changed his mind and dumped her again. Serves her right." She let out a bray of laughter.

He frowned down at her. "It's not going to be like that."

"Sure," she snorted. "I've been living here, you haven't. Plus you're like the great whatever grandson of the founder of this town and I'm...not."

Calvin studied her, his eyes glittering. "Since when do you care what people think about you?"

"I don't."

"Looks to me like you do." He moved closer until she could feel the warmth of his body burning all along hers. "People are already talking about us, June," he murmured. "They're already watching us. So let them. Have dinner with me. Let's get to know each other again."

June inhaled deeply, drew in the scent that belonged only to Calvin.

"Just dinner?" she challenged softly.

He shrugged. "We'll start with dinner," he said.

"And then we'll go to bed?"

"No." He smiled, pushing back a long lock of hair that had fallen into her face. His hand was warm and rough, and she wanted to close her eyes and nuzzle into his calloused palm. "We'll see if we have a good time. If we do, we'll go out again.

And again. And eventually, if you decide you trust me enough, maybe then..." He leaned in and breathed into her ear, "We'll see what happens."

Being this close to him was sending her up in flames. Her hands moved without volition, and she ran them up his muscled arms to his shoulders.

He shivered.

Oh, he wanted her, all right. And he might think he was going to do the noble thing, but he'd be pushing her for more as soon as that first dinner was over. Maybe even during dinner. They'd always been combustible.

"I'm different now, June," he told her. "I'm not afraid to let everyone in town know that I'm dating you."

For how long?

She didn't ask because she thought she knew the answer. Calvin might even believe what he was telling her. But once his parents and his friends got going at him again, all bets would be off.

So the real question was, what did *she* want to do?

The clear-headed, practical side of her brain told her to turn him down. She'd be a fool to go there again with this man. Yes, there would undoubtedly be gossip, but it would die away eventually if they weren't an item.

The other side of her brain...well...it had different ideas.

She'd been comparing all of the men she'd dated to him for the last fifteen years, and now he was *here*, within reach. Asking. Willing. She ran her hands over the temptation of his firm, rounded shoulders, up into his hair, and felt him shudder in response.

To taste him again, feel his body moving under hers...over hers...*in* hers...

She bit her bottom lip, sensing him watching the movement with focused intensity, even though she couldn't see the expression in those dark, dark eyes.

Oh, yeah, they'd always been combustible. The fire had burned as hot as a furnace between them. For as long as it had lasted.

What happened when he decided he was finished this time around?

She frowned.

On the other hand, who said *he* got to decide how things went?

Why couldn't she get her hands on him again, satisfy the desire that had been building up for years, and then get out? She wasn't a silly, romantic kid anymore. She could take what she wanted and move on. Maybe exorcise a few demons while she was at it. After all, there was no way it could have been as good as she remembered. Once she finally got it through her head that he was just another slobbering male, she'd be able to set the memory of Calvin aside and move on with the rest of her life.

"All right," she said at last, smoothing her hands down his chest. Big and broad and hard. *Yes.*

She was going to have some fun exorcising those demons.

He smiled as if he read her mind and liked what he saw.

"All right what?" he murmured.

She met his eyes.

"I'll go out to dinner with you."

Calvin smiled, slow and sexy in the shadows. He reached out and touched her cheek briefly, then pulled his hand away.

"When is your next night off?"

She swallowed, her mouth dry. "Tomorrow."

His eyes glowed. "Tomorrow. How about I pick you up around seven?"

June shifted, suddenly nervous. What the hell was she doing?

"Don't change your mind now," he warned. "If you back out, I'll just think you're a chicken."

She straightened. "I am not."

He shrugged, the sexy smile widening into a grin. "Bwak, bwak."

"Fine." She threw up her hands. "Seven. And you already know where I live."

"I do."

She crossed her arms, but that was a mistake because he was standing so close she brushed against his body.

"Where will you take me?" she challenged.

He rubbed the bridge of his nose. "I'll surprise you."

"In other words, you don't know."

Calvin laughed and finally took a step back. "Hell, June, I expected you to punch me when I saw you again, not agree to go out with me. I'm kind of unprepared."

She found herself reluctantly returning his smile. "If only I'd known."

He shook his head, then jerked a thumb at the Country Time. "We should go before that bartender comes looking for us."

"Oh. Right." June was surprised to realize she was disappointed. "I'll see you tomorrow, then."

He frowned. "What? I'm coming back in with you."

She had started to move past him but stopped when he spoke and stared at him. "You're coming back in?"

Calvin huffed out a breath and took her hand, tugging her towards the Country Time. "Well, of course I'm coming back in. Don't be stupid."

She pulled away. "You don't have to. And in fact, maybe we shouldn't—"

"June." Calvin propped his hands on his lean hips. "What do you think all of those people in there are going to do if I don't come back?"

"Nothing," she said, although she knew that was a lie.

He made a buzzing sound. "Wrong. They will assume you

kicked me to the curb, and will descend on you like a swarm of locusts."

She didn't say anything because he was right.

"So, I'm not going to let that happen." He reached down for her hand, brought it to his lips and kissed it, his mouth soft and warm against her skin. "I'm going to go back to the bar, talk to people, be the target of rude speculation, and smile because I know that tomorrow night I will be having dinner with the most beautiful woman in town."

Oh, he was good.

"You're going to make a fool of yourself," she said.

"I don't care. I'm not leaving you alone, June."

For how long?

Swallowing the question for the second time, June let him usher her into the building.

11

Walking back into the Country Time with June after causing such an uproar by asking her out on a date hadn't been the most comfortable thing he'd ever done in his life, Calvin reflected as he guided Big Red down the road to Ms. Gregory's house the next evening. But it had been worth it.

True, he'd felt like a beetle under a microscope for most of the night, but seeing the look of total confusion on June's face every time she'd glanced his way had been priceless. She obviously hadn't expected him to stick around, so he'd made sure he'd stayed until her shift was over.

Of course, he would have stayed anyway to be there in case some jerk, like Bernie, got in her face. Maybe it hadn't been such a great idea to approach her in front of everyone. He'd known he'd be putting himself out there, had wanted to show her he was willing to risk making an ass of himself, but he hadn't considered what it might mean for her. Which just proved that he still wasn't all that bright.

He'd offered to take her home once she was done working, but she'd slapped him away, saying she'd catch a ride with Hannah. He hadn't pushed the issue.

Not yet.

Calvin turned the pickup into Ms. Gregory's driveway and brought it to a stop in front of the garage with June's little apartment perched on top. For a moment, he sat gripping the steering wheel with both hands, surprised he was so nervous. He couldn't quite believe he was here. Taking June Esperanza out to dinner on a Saturday night again.

Why had she changed her mind about going, when it had sure looked like she was about to turn him down?

It didn't matter, he decided, turning off the engine and getting out of the truck. He'd take whatever opening she gave him.

Crickets chirped enthusiastically in the undergrowth, and the air held the heavy scent of a summer night. Calvin took a moment to fiddle with the white dress shirt he'd changed into after leaving the store, smoothing the collar before bending to shake out the crisp seams of his charcoal slacks. He couldn't stand wearing a suit jacket or tie in the heat of the summer but figured he looked presentable enough.

Reaching back into the cab, he pulled out the bouquet of flowers he'd bought for June at the florist. His father had raised his eyebrows when he'd seen them, but hadn't made any comments—just assured Calvin everything was under control as far as his mother was concerned.

Still, there'd been a hardening around his dad's mouth that said he'd heard all about the scene at the Country Time and thought he knew just what his son's plans were for the evening.

He was probably wrong about the plans, but it wasn't a surprise he knew what had happened—especially since Calvin had been forced to ask him to take care of the store that morning. There was no way he could have opened today. Two late nights in a row had taken their toll. Even mainlining caffeine wouldn't have done much to help.

At least he'd managed to get some sleep before he'd had to

go in around noon. Karen, their favorite home health aide, had been scheduled to work, and she'd come early. Better yet, she'd agreed to stay longer than normal with his mother so he could go back to bed for a while.

Karen was a local, so he was sure she'd probably heard the whole story, too. There'd been a certain twinkle in her blue eyes when she'd shooed him away, and he'd seen her hide a grin as she led his mom to the bathroom for a shower.

A rustling noise pulled him from his thoughts, and he saw an exceptionally plump squirrel hop out from behind a bush. It paused and looked at him like it was trying to decide whether or not to kick his butt. Then, apparently deciding it wasn't worth the effort, it waddled to a pole with a bird feeder hanging from the top. It slithered up the pole and jumped onto the feeder.

Calvin was surprised when the base of the feeder started spinning. He watched as the squirrel hung on with grim intent and saw it grab a handful of seed before it went flying off into the shrubbery. A moment later it was back, climbing the pole again.

Determination.

Taking a deep breath, Calvin rolled his shoulders and walked to the stairs leading to June's apartment, his stride firm. That squirrel wasn't the only one with balls around here. It was time to find out what the evening held.

He climbed the stairs easily, without strain. That was one thing he had going for him—he was still in good shape. Yes, he worked hard now at the store, but even in Philadelphia he'd been out on job sites more often than at a desk.

He wondered if June looked at him and saw a man fast approaching middle age, or if she saw the boy he'd once been.

Was she disappointed?

He got to the landing for the door to the apartment and ran

his free hand through his hair. Then he knocked quickly. Please God, just let things get started.

June opened the door right away.

He tried to speak, but no words came. She looked *amazing*.

A thin sweater clung to her luscious breasts, the burgundy color making her eyes seem somehow darker, and her skin warmer. Her midnight hair fell in thick waves over her shoulders, spilling down to those breasts, drawing his eyes. Tight black jeans, strappy high-heeled sandals, bright red toenails. *Gorgeous.*

His gaze wandered up her body again.

"Austin was right," he said when he met her eyes. She was watching him with a knowing "Mona Lisa" smile.

"About what?" she asked, quirking her eyebrows.

"You really are smoking hot."

She laughed.

"I thought you were going to stand out there all night," she taunted. "Change your mind?"

"Never." Remembering the bouquet of flowers he was holding, he gave them to her. "For you," he added, unnecessarily.

"Um, thanks." She took the flowers and bent her head to sniff them before looking up at him with a question in her eyes. "These are Gerbera daisies."

He shrugged. "They're your favorites. Or they were."

Her face closed down for a second, then she laughed. "Right. Come on in and let me put these in water."

She moved back so he could step into the room. As he closed the door behind them, she took the flowers over to the sink in her kitchenette and got a vase from a cupboard.

While she dealt with the flowers, he took the opportunity to look at her apartment. It was an open studio with a living area/kitchen at one end, and a Japanese screen partially hiding a bed at the other. There were two doors next to the bed, one of which opened to a bathroom, and the other leading to storage over the rest of garage. It was a cute, neat space, and she'd furnished it with an eclectic mix of furniture, accented with pops of color throughout.

He found himself drawn to a series of framed photographs hanging on a wall over the sofa opposite the living area's window. They were pictures of the town, the people, the woods, the mountains. He saw one that looked like the fat squirrel he'd met outside.

The photos had been altered—cropped to highlight or direct the eye, colors accented or muted, mood playful or serene. In its portrait, the squirrel sported a jaunty toupee of fluorescent pink. In a photo of Old Albert, the map of wrinkles on the man's face seemed as deep as the Grand Canyon.

"These are really good. Did you take them?" He couldn't keep the surprise out of his voice.

"Shocked?" she challenged, coming to stand next to him.

Great. He'd already offended her, and they hadn't even left her apartment yet.

"Not shocked," he hastened to assure her. "I didn't know... nobody told me you were doing this."

"Well, I guess people see me with a camera now and then, but everyone takes pictures around here. I just don't figure it's anybody's business what I do with mine."

He looked down at her and was enchanted to realize she was blushing. June, the June he'd known, had never blushed.

"Some people must know." He pointed at the portrait of Albert. "I mean, haven't you shown him that one?"

Her blush deepened. "Nah. He was out at the park sitting on a bench, and I asked if he'd mind if I took his picture. He didn't care."

Calvin's amusement fled when she mentioned the park. Where he'd dumped her.

"How do you make them look like that?" he asked, trying to bring the conversation back to more neutral territory.

June glanced at him sardonically. "I click the button," she said dryly.

He rolled his eyes. "Yeah, but they don't come out of the camera this way. You must do something to..." he gestured helplessly, "perk them up."

"Perk them up?" She laughed. "I guess I do. I'm trying to learn some software Mary Alice installed on my laptop. There's a lot you can do with digital photography if you have the tools." She sighed, sounding wistful. "I'd really like a better camera. But first I need an alternator. And a battery. And a new car."

He wanted to offer to buy her whatever she needed but kept his mouth shut. She would have thrown the suggestion back in his face and then thrown him down the stairs.

"I could keep an eye out for someone with a good deal on a used car," he said instead.

June smiled at him. "That would be great. As long as it's not Claude. I've learned my lesson there."

"Some lessons are hard to learn," he said. He'd meant it to be sort of a joke, but the words fell flat, and they stared at each other.

June shifted, breaking the moment.

"Are you taking me to dinner or not?"

Calvin relaxed. "Yes," he said.

Her expression turned suspicious. "Where are we going anyway?"

He smiled slightly. "You'll find out when we get there."

June considered him, then shrugged and turned to get her purse from the small kitchen table.

"Well, it's your own fault if I'm not dressed right," she said, pulling the strap over her shoulder.

"You're fine."

He followed her across the room and waited a few steps down the stairway outside while she closed and locked the door. The position gave him a great view of her exceptional ass, which she realized when she caught him staring at it. She scowled at him, and he grinned back at her, unrepentant.

"Move along." June waved her hand imperiously, her fingernails painted to match her toes. He wanted to pull her close, hold her hips, and roll his face against her belly. He thought she might have realized it, because her face sobered, and she watched him with an intent expression. Calvin balled his hands into fists to keep from grabbing her, then turned and made his way down the stairs.

At the bottom, he opened Big Red's passenger door, holding it so she could slide into the truck before closing it gently behind her. He walked around and climbed up behind the wheel, turning the key to start the engine. At the growl of sound, he felt himself settle. The night was finally about to begin.

"Ms. Gregory is away for a couple of days visiting a friend in New York City," June said suddenly.

Calvin wondered what that had to do with anything.

"Good for her." He put the vehicle in gear and backed up into the turnaround so he could head down the driveway, anxious to get underway.

"So, I guess I'm all alone here tonight," she said innocently.

Calvin drew in a sharp breath at the invitation he thought he heard in her voice. Or was that just wishful thinking?

"You're not alone," he said, trying to speak lightly as he turned onto the road. "I met your guardian outside in the garden before he got thrown off the bird feeder."

"Who...? Oh, the squirrel." Her eyes were sparkling with laughter when he glanced at her, and he took another hard breath. "That thing is determined to figure out the bird feeder. I think it will, too."

"I saw it swipe some seed before it went flying," he told her.

"I'm not surprised." She shook her head, and her long, dark

hair brushed his shoulder. "The squirrels always beat Ms. Gregory's 'squirrel proof' feeders."

"She should just stop feeding the birds."

"She's stubborn." June stared out the windshield. "And why should she give up something she enjoys?"

Calvin had a feeling she wasn't just talking about Ms. Gregory and her squirrels, but June seemed disinclined to continue. He tried to think of a generic topic of conversation that wasn't related to the weather or business, came up empty, and turned on the radio instead. Soon, mellow jazz filled the cab of the truck.

12

June didn't come out of her reverie until Calvin turned off the highway and onto the road running past the lake. She sat straighter, looking around.

"The Fallside?" she asked, turning to him. "Really?"

"We're on a date, aren't we?" He felt defensive. "I wanted to take you someplace nice."

The Fallside Restaurant was housed in an elegant old mill set beside the bank of waterfalls named after Calvin's ancestor. The restaurant had a reputation for gourmet, expensive food served in tiny portions and was usually booked weeks in advance.

Calvin had managed to get a last-minute reservation by pulling some strings with the owner, who was looking for a deal on slate flooring. The Fallside wasn't exactly his style, but he remembered how June had always talked about going there and splurging on a meal. He'd thought it would be a good place to take her for their first date.

Well, their second first date.

"Goddamnit," June swore, and he looked over at her in surprise.

"What?"

"Why didn't you tell me you were taking me to Fallside? I'm not dressed right."

"You look fine," he said, honestly confused. Hell, she looked more than just "fine." She looked incredible.

June frowned at him and tugged at her pants. "I am wearing *jeans.*"

Amused, he reached over and patted her hand. "I won't let them throw you out."

"Thanks," she muttered and threw herself back in the seat.

He pulled into the parking lot and stopped the truck in an empty spot. The old mill and the tall trees surrounding it sparkled under a blanket of little white lights in the summer evening, while the rumble of the Hardy Falls thundered in the background.

"You do realize everyone in town is going to know you brought me here," she said suddenly.

He turned to face her more fully. "Yes." That had been part of the plan.

She studied him, then smiled. "Don't say I didn't warn you."

He touched her hair before pulling back. "Stay where you are so I can open your door for you," he ordered.

She rolled her eyes. "Woof."

Grinning, he got out of the truck and jogged around to get her door. He offered a hand to help her descend, which earned him another eye-roll, but she took it.

"Come on," he said, tugging gently. "We have reservations."

She said something under her breath that sounded like "Christ," but let him escort her to the glittering building. Inside the front doors, a tall, slender hostess dressed in an elegant black dress stood behind a podium. She gave them a cold, professional smile that did not move much of her exquisitely made-up face.

"Yes, sir?" she asked Calvin politely.

"We have reservations," he answered. "Hardy. Seven thirty."

The young woman swept them with a comprehensive gaze that took in his lack of a jacket and tie, as well as June's jeans, but she inclined her head. The owner really wanted that flooring.

"Follow me."

She gathered up two leather-bound menus and led June and Calvin through the crowded restaurant to a small table by one of the plate glass windows that had been installed in the old building to give patrons a view of the lake. Calvin cursed under his breath when he saw that he and June were attracting quite a bit of attention from the other diners as they made their way across the room.

"Your server will be with you shortly." The hostess gave them another cold smile. "Enjoy your visit."

"Sure," June said and sat down before Calvin could pull out her chair. He sighed and took his seat on the other side of the table.

"I feel like I'm on a laboratory slide." She cast a glance around the room.

"I'm sure they're just scandalized by the way we're dressed." His shoulders wanted to twitch from the sensation of being the object of so much covert attention.

June leaned towards him. "Listen, why don't we just blow this popsicle stand? Get up and leave." She was whispering as if prison guards would overhear them planning an escape.

He frowned at her. "I'm showing you a good time, damn it."

"Don't look now, but I think you're trying too hard."

His frown deepened. "I've never walked out of a restaurant once I was seated." And he'd gone to a lot of trouble to get this reservation. The deal he'd given the owner was going to hurt.

"Suit yourself." June sank back in her chair and glowered at a bright-eyed woman wearing a dress in an unfortunate shade of mauve who was intently watching them from another table.

"That's Margo Truelove. If she comes over here, I'm going to stab her in the head. No, I'll stab her in her tongue. That would have more impact."

Calvin patted her hand. "Easy there, tiger."

A young man dressed in the stark black uniform of The Fallside wait staff walked up to their table, interrupting June mid-growl.

"Good evening, my name is Brandon, and I'll be taking care of you tonight," he said in a monotone voice, sounding bored out of his mind. "Can I start you off with a drink?" He held up his order pad and looked completely uninterested in their decision.

June ordered a gin and tonic. Calvin asked for a bottle of beer because he didn't like the brands they had on tap. Brandon sneered at the request, but dutifully wrote it down and left.

"You know better than to order bottled beer in a place like this," June chided, opening her menu. "You should have learned that in Philly. Holy cow, check out the price of the lobster."

"I learned a lot in Philly." Calvin opened his own menu. "And I order whatever I damn well please, as long as it's available."

June looked at him, her eyes big and dark in the light of the sun reflecting off the lake outside the window.

"And what do you think is available tonight?" she asked, voice soft.

He considered her carefully before he spoke. "I thought we could talk tonight," he said finally. "Get to know each other again."

She was silent for a moment, then closed her menu and put it aside. "Why would you want to do that?"

Calvin reached over the table to run a finger down the back of her hand. "Because I've missed you." *So much.*

June sat back and pulled her hand away. "And you really thought we could talk here?" She glared at Margo Truelove again. "You must have been out of your mind."

Before Calvin could respond, Brandon came with their drink orders. He placed them carefully on the table, then straightened and stood with his order pad, pen raised ostentatiously.

"Have you decided?" he asked in the same bored voice.

Calvin looked at the kid and realized June was right. This whole thing had been a mistake. He'd wanted to show her he valued her, but they couldn't talk here. Not the way they needed to, not in this highbrow, stuffy restaurant with the eyes of the town watching and the ears of the town listening. He had been trying too hard to prove himself.

He turned to June.

"Did you mean it when you said we should just leave?" One of the many things he'd learned during his time away was, if you screwed up, you didn't let it fester. You fixed it as soon as possible. On the other hand, he didn't want to piss June off by dragging her out of the place.

She cocked her head. "Yes," she said. "Trying to have dinner with everyone watching us is going to screw with my digestion."

"So you wouldn't mind if we got out of here?"

June grinned at him, picked up her gin and tonic, and took a large gulp.

"Nope."

"We need the check," he said to Brandon.

"Wh...what?" the boy gaped, the first real expression he'd shown.

"You know what? Never mind." Calvin pulled out his wallet and threw a twenty and a ten on the table. Should be more than enough to cover the drinks, even in a fancy place like this. "Come on," he said to June, standing and holding out a hand to her.

To his surprise, she actually took it and, still grinning, let him propel her to the door while the other customers watched with open-mouthed interest. June's whole body shook with laughter as she kept pace.

When they jogged past the hostess, the woman's cold face cracked with horror, her eyes opening so wide they were in danger of falling out of her head.

"Sir!" she called after them.

Calvin ignored her and tugged June out the front door into the warm evening. Still holding her hand, he ran with her to Big Red, feeling young and reckless and alive for the first time since he was twenty-four.

They both jumped into the truck, and the powerful engine started with a roar. Putting it in gear, he drove out of the parking lot and headed back down the lake road.

"Did you...see...the hostess?" June gasped. "Her face..." She dissolved into giggles, clutching her belly.

Calvin smirked at her.

"I don't think anyone's ever walked out of there before," he mused.

"I'm pretty sure we didn't walk out—we ran." June panted for a moment, getting herself under control. "What are we going to do now?"

He didn't know. "There are a couple of chain restaurants along the interstate," he said. "Or fast food?"

"Some date," she chuckled.

The sun was starting to set, the light strong coming in through the windshield, dazzling his eyes until he put on his sunglasses. He glanced at June and found her watching him.

Suddenly, he knew where he wanted to go. He turned down another gravel road to drive around the lake instead of continuing to the highway. June drew in a breath at the change of direction, but she didn't protest. He thought that was a good sign.

The park at Hardy Falls Lake had a name, but nobody in town ever remembered it. It was just "the park." It was a popular place for families, but Calvin brought Big Red to a stop along the side of the road at the upper end where nobody really went.

Grass and trees flowed down a slight hill to the lakefront, and The Fallside could be seen perched on the opposite shore. Sailboats bobbed out on the water, with ducks and geese paddling in the currents. A blue heron flew past, its long neck curved up and back in a sharp "s."

June didn't say anything, so Calvin jumped out of the truck and reached behind the seat to grab the old blanket he had stuffed back there in case he needed to protect furniture or something. Bundling it up under his arm, he walked around to open the passenger door. June sat in her seat, watching him.

He hesitated, not sure what she was thinking.

"Do you want to go?" he asked uncertainly.

She was silent for another moment.

"No," she said and jumped out of the truck. "But I am not ruining these new shoes by getting stuck in the mud," she added as he closed the door behind her.

He looked down at the sexy, strappy sandals with the mile-high heels and swallowed.

"I'll carry you," he croaked.

June turned her eyes up to heaven, then bent down and slipped off the shoes. She straightened, holding them with a finger through the straps, and gestured ironically.

"After you."

He found himself mesmerized by her red toenails and bare, narrow feet, staring at them until she coughed out a laugh.

"Oh. Sorry."

Turning, he picked his way to a spot where the grass was thick and soft before being taken over by pebbles closer to the shore. He spread the blanket and sat; June plopped down next to him. She tossed her shoes aside and leaned back on her hands, crossing her ankles out in front of her, the warm wind blowing through her long, loose hair.

They didn't say anything for a few minutes, just listened to the noise of the geese and ducks, the humming of the bees in the wildflowers, the constant noise of the waterfall. There were a few families further down the shore where an elaborate playground had been set up, and Calvin could hear the screams of children playing. A typical, lazy summer evening.

They were alone.

"It looks nice from here," June said at last, indicating The Fallside, its myriad white lights reflecting in the water. "It looks like a nice, old building. You can't tell everyone in the place has a stick up their butt."

He grimaced.

"Yeah, sorry about that. I just wanted you to have a good time, and I remembered you'd always said you wanted to eat there."

"Well, I have eaten there. Several times, as a matter of fact." She looked over at him. "I've been living here a while now, you know."

"Yes." He frowned. It was a sobering thought. Someone else had taken her to The Fallside for the first time. And the second. It was a reminder that things weren't the same now as they'd been before.

"Times change," she said, channeling his thoughts.

"I know." He turned to her and took off the sunglasses so he could see her better. "There's a lot I don't know about you."

"You think?" June rolled her head back, looked up at the sky. "I'm pretty much an open book. Not much chance of keeping secrets in this town."

"I didn't know you took photographs."

She stacked her bare feet on top of each other, waggled them back and forth. "Well, don't beat yourself up about that one. Not many people know. I told Hannah and Mary Alice, but that's about it."

He ran his eyes down the line of her body.

So beautiful.

"I don't know why you're here," he said. "I don't know why you didn't just shoot me when you saw me again."

She smiled up at the sky, then looked at him.

"Maybe I wanted to, and I held myself back. I'm getting mellow in my old age."

He returned her smile, and their eyes locked. Abruptly, June pulled herself up into a cross-legged position. She plucked idly at a loose string on the blanket, watching him.

"Talk about not knowing—I'm still not sure why you're interested in picking things up with me again," she said. "Seems like that ship sailed."

He sat up and faced her, crossing his legs so their knees bumped.

"You can't figure it out? Then you must have forgotten how we were."

She scowled at him. "Just because we were that way once doesn't mean we'll be that way now."

"No." He looked down, wondering how he could explain. Neither of them was who they'd been. "I want another chance, June."

She shrugged. "Then we should have stayed at my place and gotten naked."

"I want more than just sex."

She quirked her eyebrows at him. "No sex?"

"I didn't say *no* sex. I said I want *more* than just sex. We used to have more."

"We used to have a lot. But then you decided you didn't want it anymore."

"That's not true."

She laughed without humor, waving away an interested

bee. "You were pretty clear, Calvin. I don't know what it was you were looking for, but it sure as hell wasn't me."

Calvin picked up a leaf that had blown onto the blanket, twirling the stem between his fingers. How could he explain something he was still figuring out himself?

"I wanted you, but I got confused," he said slowly. "I believed what people told me." Especially since two of those people had been his own mother and father.

Her lips thinned. "They told you I was a slut."

"They told me that I didn't want to stay, that I needed to go, that my life wasn't here," he said, although she was right about the other. He shook his head. "I was just...I just believed them after a while. I didn't know what I wanted until I didn't have it anymore. And then it was too late."

She turned her head to look out over the lake to The Fallside.

"But now you're back," she said.

"Yes."

"I don't know if I can trust anything you're telling me," she said after a long pause, still not looking at him. "For all I know, you're just trying to see if you can relive your misspent youth or something. Maybe you've decided that since you're going to be stuck here, you might as well have a friend to help pass the time."

His stomach clutched, and he let the leaf drop. "Is that really what you think about me?" he asked. Because if it was— if she had that poor of an opinion of him—he would back off now.

"Maybe." She slid a glance his way. "No," she admitted, and he muffled a sigh of relief. "But..." she looked at The Fallside again, "when you left, Calvin, it hurt."

"I'm sorry, June." He clenched his hands into fists so he wouldn't reach for her, because he sensed she didn't want him touching her now.

"And when I found out you'd gotten married, it hurt worse." She met his eyes, the expression in her own determined. "So don't expect me to just go jumping into the deep end with you again and being all committed and everything. If we go there this time, it's strictly for fun, get it? You walk away, I walk away, and we're good, okay? Those are the ground rules."

Now his insides churned for a different reason. The thought of June walking away was not a pleasant one.

"I've already told you, I'm not leaving."

"Sure." She shrugged, and he could tell she didn't believe him. "But if you change your mind, it's fine. No strings attached."

He wanted the damned strings. But he also knew his words wouldn't mean anything to her. He'd have to prove himself by his actions.

"We'll have trouble beating our first date though, huh?" he said, deliberately changing the subject.

June laughed and relaxed. It was only then he realized how tense she'd been.

"The night's still young," she said, glancing at him coyly.

"We could go for ribs," he said, wishing he'd thought to bring a picnic with him. The lake was beautiful, but he was getting hungry. "I heard about a great place that's not too far from here."

June reached over and knocked her fist on his arm. "Now you're talking." Her stomach growled in agreement, and they both laughed.

She pushed herself up to stand on the blanket looking down at him.

"Get moving," she ordered. "You owe me dinner." She picked up her shoes and strode back to the truck.

Before he stood, he watched her walk away. Then he gathered up the blanket and followed.

13

Later, after they'd lingered over huge plates of ribs in a cute restaurant June had not even known existed, Calvin drove her home in his big pickup truck. She watched the headlights track along the darkened road, feeling pleasantly satiated and a lot more comfortable than she'd expected to be when she'd gotten dressed for the evening. It had been surprisingly nice to spend time with him again.

Uh oh. Don't go there.

Instead, June focused on the upgrade her closet might get out of the evening.

There was actually a surprising amount of storage space for her tiny apartment because the door next to her bathroom led to an attic over the other half of Ms. Gregory's spacious garage. June was allowed to put whatever she wanted in there, but it was completely unorganized and had a second entrance around back to give Ms. Gregory access. Which meant it wasn't exactly private.

Since she never knew when her landlady or a random contractor might need to get into the area, she kept her day-to-day clothes and other essentials in a stand-alone wardrobe in her bedroom area. That was fine, but it took up a lot of space she didn't have.

When she'd casually mentioned the problem to Calvin over dinner, his eyes had lit up at the challenge. Before she knew what was happening, he was drawing a plan on a paper napkin to show her how they might be able to add some walls and split the storage space to give her a dedicated walk-in closet.

The back door was her second exit in case of a fire, but he'd said they could put in a steel door between her area and Ms. Gregory's. Then she could leave the door in the apartment open without worrying about security or privacy.

"It looks great," June had said, gazing longingly at the lines he'd drawn on the napkin. She'd been able to see how it could be done, damn him, and the thought of having a real closet had made her salivate. "But there's no way Ms. Gregory will put out the money for this." Her landlady was wonderful and kind, but she could pinch a penny until it screamed.

"I'll talk to her." Calvin tucked the napkin into the pocket of his slacks. "I should be able to give her a discount on supplies."

"Because you're trying to get in good with me?" she'd teased.

He'd looked at her with dark and sober eyes. "Because you're my friend," he'd corrected gently.

But they weren't friends, June thought now, breathing in the night air wafting through the truck's partially open windows. They were something, but they weren't friends.

Still, it had been illuminating to watch him work, drawing on the napkin with quick, deft strokes, coming up with angles and ratios and who knew what else without using a calculator. She'd always been hopeless at math beyond what it took to figure out checks and tips. It really must have been hard for him to give up his career in Philadelphia.

Because he'd wanted to come home.

For his parents, she reminded herself. Not for her.

Which was good. This time around, she was all about having some fun. Dinners out, sex, and a few laughs. No expectations.

And maybe a closet.

"Those were good ribs," she said, breaking the comfortable silence they'd maintained since leaving the restaurant. "I can't believe you didn't get any sauce on your shirt." He'd inhaled his food, almost eaten the plate it had been served on, but his shirt was still spotless and white.

"Fast but neat." He glanced at her, face shadowed in the ambient light from the dashboard. "Martin Scanner told me about that place the other day, but that was the first time I'd been there. I'm glad it lived up to the press." He laughed. "If you ever want to find out about restaurants, just ask the Four Musketeers."

"We should have gone there first, instead of starting out at The Fallside."

"Yeah." His mouth twisted. "Sorry about that." They drove in silence for another moment. "So, uh, who took you to The Fallside the first time?" he asked.

His voice was so casual she almost laughed out loud but caught herself in time.

"I'm not sure. I think it was Noah Chertok."

Calvin frowned. "Noah Chertok, the contractor?"

"Yes, that's him." June looked at Calvin and bit back another laugh. Somebody was *not* happy about her having gone out with Noah. "If I remember right, I had told him I'd always wanted to go to The Fallside, so he arranged it as a surprise for my birthday the year we were dating."

"Oh." The single word was brittle.

Suddenly, June wasn't amused anymore. She turned to watch the trees flowing past the window, leaves silvery in the light of the moon that had risen while they'd been dawdling over ribs. She'd forgotten until just now that Calvin had promised to take her to The Fallside for her twenty-fourth birthday.

He hadn't stayed in town that long.

"The next time I went there was the year Hannah turned twenty-one and I turned thirty," she said, just to say something. "Kind of a joint celebration."

"Did Chertok go, too?" Calvin asked, voice biting.

"No. We were finished by then." None of the relationships she'd had after Calvin had lasted very long, not until she'd started seeing Pat. And look at how well that had worked out.

"Good."

June rested back against the headrest. "You should have heard Fred when Hannah and I told him we were both going to be off the same Friday night."

She chuckled at the memory, rolling her head so she could see Calvin. "Even *I'd* never heard some of the words he was using. I think that night was the first time Fred had worked since Hannah graduated from high school. Probably the last time, too. He never let us forget it."

"Fred was a dick," Calvin said, turning the truck onto June's road, holding the steering wheel loosely with his big, capable hands.

June shivered. She'd always loved his hands.

"I stayed in town for Hannah, not Fred," she said abruptly, angry that just watching him drive made her want to jump him.

"Well, I know *that*," he said. The unmistakable "duh" in his voice settled her down.

She shrugged. "Just thought I'd put it out there. There've been a lot of rumors over the years saying Fred and I were lovers. We never were."

He glanced at her and seemed puzzled. "I know, June. You would never have given Fred Frederickson the time of day."

"Because he was older?" she pushed.

"Because he was an asshole," he told her. "I know those

rumors weren't true. Fred probably started them himself when you turned him down."

She'd always thought so, too. Hearing him echo her feelings surprised her into silence. That, and the relief of finding out he didn't believe what people had said about her.

"He approached me," she heard herself saying. "I told him I wasn't interested." And the rumors about her moral character had heated up shortly afterward.

Calvin nodded. "There you go," he said as he maneuvered the truck into Ms. Gregory's driveway.

The elderly librarian's neat, white house was dark, but June had left a lamp on over her apartment's front door so yellow light spilled down the stairs and out over the yard. Calvin parked and turned off the engine before facing her, his arm across the back of the seat, the warmth of his body curling around her skin.

"You're home," he said.

All at once, the cab of the truck seemed very small. June reached up and touched his cheek, letting the bristles of his whiskers tickle her palm. She smoothed her fingers over his mouth and chin, over the creases that were the evidence of the years they'd been apart.

Neither one of them were children any longer. They could take what they wanted.

She breathed deeply, drew in the scent of his skin, her breasts swelling to brush against his hard chest in the confined space.

"I'm home," she agreed, voice husky. "Now what are you going to do?" The words were taunting, teasing him. She felt him pull in air and let it out slowly, his arm an iron band behind her.

"I'm going to kiss you good night," he said, sounding strangled. "Then I'm going to watch you walk up the stairs to your apartment."

"You are?" she murmured. She leaned into him and spoke into his ear. "Are you sure?"

She was close enough to see him swallow. Hard.

"I am. Damn it," he added. "Then I'm going to go home and jack off in the shower."

June's breath stuttered at the mental image.

His hard body. The wetness of the water. His hand moving desperately over his erection, striving for a climax.

"I think I have a better idea."

She kissed him, attacking his mouth with all of her pent-up passion. He opened for her, and she tasted ribs, and beer, and Calvin.

He wrapped his arms around her and returned the kiss for several long moments before pushing her back. They panted, staring at each other.

"No," he said.

"No?" She wound her fingers around his ears, and he shuddered.

"We can't...this isn't...I don't..." he wasn't making much sense. It gave her hope that his resolve was cracking.

"We can." She kissed him. "This is." Kiss. "We will." She went for his mouth again.

His hands moved down her back, over her hips, shifting her until she was riding his knee. She rocked against it, using the hardness to apply pressure where she needed it the most.

"Not tonight," he said breathlessly before running his mouth over her cheek and down her neck. "Show you... respect..." He kissed her again.

"Respect me in the morning," she said when she could speak. "Fuck me tonight."

He jerked and pulled back.

"I want to make love to you, June," he said seriously. "It's more than just fucking."

She stopped trying to get closer and looked into his eyes, dark as wells in the dim light.

"I don't know what I want," she told him.

"I know. That's why—"

"Except I want you to come upstairs with me tonight."

He drew in a deep, shaky breath. "Trust me, I'd really, really love to."

"Well, then—"

"But we're not ready. *You're* not ready. It's too early."

"I'm ready!" She tugged his hair hard, frustrated that he was treating her as if she didn't know her own mind. "I'm not a child. I'm really fucking ready!"

He kissed her again, slicked his tongue against hers, rocked his erection against her stomach, and then broke away, gasping.

"You don't trust me."

"What the hell do you want from me?" she wailed, desperate in a way only he could make her. "Undying love? That's not going to happen. So just come on upstairs and screw me into the mattress, will you?"

He practically shoved her away from him. Pushing back into his own seat, he faced forward again, gripped the steering wheel, and then rested his forehead on it. He let out a long, low, laughing groan.

"Christ, June. You are killing me."

"Then come on." She was so hot she was burning up.

He lifted his head to look at her. "I don't put out on a first date." His voice held equal measures pain and amusement.

"I'm out of here." June grabbed the door handle, ready to rip it off its hinges. Here she was, practically throwing herself at the man, and he made her feel like a total jackass. What the hell kind of game was he playing?

"June." He grabbed her shoulders when she would have jumped out, holding her in place. "There is nothing I would like to do more than come up to that apartment with you," he whispered in her ear.

"Too late now," she snarled at him.

"But it's too soon," he said, rubbing his cheek in her hair. "For both of us."

Not for her. The sooner she got over him, the better off she'd be.

"I'll pick you up around one o'clock tomorrow," he said. "We can have some lunch before you go to work."

"Go to hell," she snapped, just as she had the night her car had broken down.

"Nope." He ran his lips over the place where her neck met her shoulder before pulling back with a sigh. "You'd better get out of here."

June flung herself out of the truck and marched to the stairs. Behind her, she heard the engine start and rev.

"June," Calvin called over the noise. "If you try to run away, I will find you."

She called him a name that made him laugh.

But he didn't drive away until she was safely upstairs in her apartment.

14

Two weeks later, June decided that Calvin was trying to drive her insane.

She prowled restlessly around her small apartment, pausing at the window to watch the fat squirrel hanging on the bird feeder. As the feeder spun, the squirrel held on to the perch with one paw and used the other to dig into an opening, shoveling birdseed to the ground. Then it let go, flew off the feeder, and scurried over to eat the seed it had dumped.

Perseverance paid off.

Calvin's sure had.

Somehow she seemed to have been dating him for the past two weeks, although she still wasn't quite sure how it had happened.

He'd shown up promptly at one o'clock the day after their first date, just like he'd said he would. Rather than telling him to go jump off a cliff, as she'd fully intended, she'd found herself going out to lunch with the man.

Afterward, he'd driven her to work before going back to the hardware store. Then he'd come into the Country Time that evening, sitting at the bar as bold as you please, refusing to acknowledge the whispers swirling around about how they'd run out of The Fallside the night before.

June had tried to ignore him, she really had. But she found there wasn't much you could do when Calvin wanted your attention. She'd even been kind of disappointed when he'd said he couldn't stay until the end of her shift and had left around nine.

That had set up a routine of sorts. At one point or another during her day, she saw Calvin. Either he took her to lunch, or he came into the Country Time after he knocked off at the hardware store. Often, it was both.

Before her car was fixed, he'd driven her to or from work. Now that she was the proud owner of a new alternator, new battery, and new power steering lines, she didn't need to depend on him for transportation, but he still came into the Country Time almost every night.

When she'd had a day off, he'd taken her to the multiplex in the next town, and they'd seen the latest blockbuster superhero movie. He'd remembered how much she hated chick flicks, shared his tub of popcorn, and had about busted a gut laughing when she cursed out the superhero's girlfriend for being an idiot.

She was having fun, June realized, staring out at the gardens she still had not photographed. It just wasn't the sort of fun she'd expected.

She'd been pretty sure she'd be having sex by now. That had been the point of going out with Calvin, after all. Instead, her head was probably going to explode from the pressure of unrequited lust.

There was definitely heat between them, and they'd indulged in some passionate make out sessions in the front seat of his truck over the past couple of days. But every time she'd tried to force the issue, he'd pulled away, told her it was too soon, and that she wasn't ready.

He kept insisting she didn't know her own mind or feelings, but June suspected he was the one who had the problem. He was treating her like she was as much of a victim as the superhero's girlfriend in the movie.

Time to show him he was wrong.

It was her night off again, and Calvin had made arrangements to pick her up and take her to the rib joint they'd tried on their first date. That's what he thought was going to happen, anyway. He was in for a surprise.

June smiled and looked at the clock. It was finally time to get ready.

She was going to hit him with both barrels.

Still smiling, she headed for the bathroom.

～

Calvin decided he would die of blue balls. The woman was driving him crazy.

Of course, it was his own fault, he admitted as he said goodbye to Toby, the hardware store's other part-time employee, and headed out to where Big Red sat in the parking lot. June had tried to push their relationship several times over the past couple of weeks, but he was determined to wait.

He wasn't sure how much longer that determination was going to hold, though. He'd wanted her for a very long time; being around her every day like this made his whole body ache.

His plan was working, he reminded himself, climbing into the truck and starting the engine. June was beginning to relax around him. They'd had a chance to talk, flirt, date, and get to know each other again.

Even the townspeople, after much speculation about the aborted dinner at The Fallside, had started to back off, seeming to accept that they would see June and Calvin in each other's company. Not that it mattered, but it would make things easier if they could go out to dinner without causing a scandal.

A few minutes after leaving the hardware store, Calvin pulled into the driveway of his parents' graceful, old farmhouse, intending to shower and change before heading out to pick up June for their date. Whistling, he jumped out of the truck and jogged up the front steps, opening the door and letting himself inside.

He stopped short when he saw his mother standing in the hallway.

"Mom?" He walked to her, kissed her on one soft cheek. "It's six o'clock. Aren't you hungry?" His mom's routine was very important to her.

"I was waiting for you," she said. "I thought we could eat together."

Calvin shifted. "Um, I'm going out tonight, Mom."

"Oh." She blinked rapidly, as if trying to process the information. "But I waited."

"I know." His heart broke, just a little bit. June would understand, wouldn't she? "I'll just call—"

"Are you seeing that woman?" she snapped in one of those lightning-fast mood swings she sometimes experienced. "That slut?"

He stiffened. "I don't—"

"I've told you before that I don't want you spending time with her." His mother crossed her arms over her thin chest. "You're heading out of town soon anyway. It's not like you're going to be here much longer."

Oh, God. She thought it was fifteen years ago. They'd fought then, more than once. She'd been very vocal about June not being good enough for him. Now he knew it was the opposite—he would never be good enough for June.

"Mom," he said, as gently as he could, "I'm going out to dinner and—"

"No!" she shrieked. "I mean it, Calvin Ronald Hardy. You will not."

He tried to hang onto his patience.

"Mom, you really can't tell me what to do."

"What's going on?"

Calvin sighed in relief when his father came through the kitchen door.

"Eva?" Ronald watched his wife with concern. "Aren't you hungry? You need to eat so you can get ready for bed."

"What?" Calvin's mother put a hand to her forehead. "I'm hungry."

"Then go on and eat, dear," his father said.

She blinked at him. "Where?"

"I'll show you." Ronald put his arm around her shoulders, then looked at Calvin. "I'll be right back."

"Okay." Calvin stood in the hallway, clasping and unclasping his hands until his father returned.

"I have to get back to her. She can't remember how to use a fork."

Calvin heaved out a sigh. "Do you want me to cancel my plans? I'll call June and—"

"No." His father shook his head. "You go on. If you're here, she'll just be more upset."

"I thought she was good today. When I walked in, she looked almost normal."

Calvin's dad smiled without humor. "She's been off and on all afternoon. That aide, the new one? She was gossiping about you and June. I think it set her off."

Calvin dragged a hand through his hair. "I don't get it!" he exclaimed in frustration. "Why does she hate June so much?" His mother had always been extremely clear about how she felt.

"I don't—"

There was a sudden, loud crash of crockery in the other room, and they both sprinted for the kitchen.

Calvin stopped just inside the door, while his father hurried to his mother's side. She was standing in the middle of the floor, shards of a broken plate and spilled food scattered around her feet.

She looked at them, eyes confused. "I was trying to clean up."

"Just stay right there, Eva," Ronald said. "You haven't eaten yet, dear, so you don't need to clean up."

"Oh. Okay."

She remained obediently still as Ronald went for a broom. Calvin got the dustpan and brush from the kitchen closet and bent down to brush up the debris, while his father returned with the broom and carefully swept up the smaller pieces. When it was safe for her to move, Calvin's dad led his mother back to her chair and convinced her to sit down.

"Dad," Calvin said, "Really, I can call June and—"

"No." His father cut him off, putting a hand on Eva's shoulder. "Go. It will be best if it's just her and me tonight."

"Are you sure?"

"I am."

Still troubled, feeling guilty as hell, Calvin walked over to the table and bent down to kiss his mother. She screeched and pulled away.

"Who are you? I don't know you."

Sighing, Calvin straightened. "We're going to have to talk, Dad," he said.

His father shook his head. "Just go."

Calvin left his parents alone. As quickly as he could, he showered, shaved, and changed, then headed downstairs again.

When he passed the kitchen door, he saw his mom was sitting at the table, calmly eating a bowl of cereal. Every time she dipped the spoon into the bowl, she seemed to forget what to do with it. His father gently moved her hand, pressed the spoon against her lips.

"Like this, honey."

Calvin watched them for a few minutes, then went out. He jumped into Big Red, started the engine, and headed for the highway. He needed to be away from there. He needed June; needed to hold onto her and forget everything else for a little while.

The drive seemed to take forever, but eventually he turned into Ms. Gregory's driveway and pulled up in front of the garage. He took the stairs two at a time to the landing at June's apartment.

She opened the door as soon as he knocked. For a moment he simply stared at her, all of the blood in his body racing to his dick so quickly it made him lightheaded. *Holy shit.*

June was wearing a very, *very* short red dress with silk stockings, red garters, and matching shoes sporting high, spiky heels. Her hair was loose, her eyes dark and smoky, and her mouth, painted the same murderous red as the dress and shoes, quirked as she smiled up at him.

"Why, hello Calvin," she said, her voice low and sultry. "Fancy meeting you—" she broke off, and the smile fell away. "What's wrong?"

"Nothing." He walked into the apartment, shut the door, and drew her into his arms for a long kiss. The taste of her, the smell of her skin under the bewitching perfume she wore, centered him.

He and his father would still have to talk, he still had to face some difficult decisions. But here was June, burning like a flame in his arms. He kissed her again, deeper this time. When he finally let her back away, they were both gasping for air.

"I thought we were going out," he panted, trying to remind himself and his blue balls about the game plan.

Doesn't believe you...needs to trust you...

"Fuck that."

For one crazed moment, he thought his abused manhood had actually spoken, but then he realized it had been June. He stared at her, his mind still fuzzy from the kiss, and she pressed her body closer. That didn't help his ability to focus.

"June," he said. "You need to—"

"No," she said firmly, her dark eyes glinting with determination. "Not this time. You are not leaving me hanging again."

"I just..."

His words died when she rubbed herself against him like a cat, ran her fingers through his hair, and pulled his head down to hers.

"I want you," she whispered against his mouth, and kissed him.

He responded, couldn't help but respond, and found himself clutching her hips, kneading them through the silky fabric of that wicked dress.

"I want you, too," he wheezed when she let go of his mouth and started unbuttoning his shirt. "But I...Christ, June!" She licked his skin, pulled it up against her teeth, sucked in a way guaranteed to leave a hickey. "I want you," he repeated, "but—"

"No." She held his face in both her hands and glared up at him. "There is no 'but' tonight. We are having sex tonight."

"June—" She'd said "sex," not "make love."

Abruptly, she pushed him away and walked over to the window, staring out at the evening sunlight before turning to face him again.

"What do you expect from me, Calvin?" she demanded. "Do you think I'm going to magically turn into that twenty-three-year-old girl again? Ready to jump when you say so? Because that's not going to happen."

"No, I—"

"Or maybe you just think you know best," she said, talking over him. "That it all has to go exactly the way you decide it should. I've been asking for more from you for days, but you don't think it's the time so you back off, even though it's obvious we both want to go there. I'm tired of it."

He tensed. "June—"

"If you don't want this," she gestured between them, "that's fine. Just say it already and go have a good life. But stop jerking me around because you don't trust me."

He stared. She thought *he* didn't trust *her*? But everything he'd done had been to convince *her* to trust *him*.

Right?

"You can't force this, Calvin," June said, more quietly. "It might never be what you think it should be." She tilted her head to the side, and her dark hair drifted over her shoulder. "But I want you now. I want you in my bed. Isn't that enough for tonight?"

Calvin realized that he'd been trying to keep control of the situation. And if he wanted June, he was going to have to let that control go. If he kept pushing her for something she wasn't ready to give, he was going to lose her.

He would have to go even further out on a limb than he'd thought. Getting kicked to the curb in front of the whole town would be the least of his worries if he let her in, but she kept him out.

Oh, who the hell was he kidding? She was already in.

He took a step toward her, then another, walking until he stood directly in front of her. She didn't move, didn't lift her arms to him. She just watched him through deep, fathomless eyes.

"It's enough," he said. "It's more than enough."

He bent his head, she lifted hers, and they kissed.

It was a soft kiss at first—tender, almost a promise. But it soon deepened, heating up to damned near scorching. Calvin moved closer, then closer still. He wrapped himself around her lithe body, pulled her tighter into the cradle of his thighs, and used his mouth to ravish her lips, her neck, her face.

June's hands were busy. He could feel her unbuttoning his shirt the rest of the way and pulling it out of his khakis. While he ran his teeth along her collarbone, she pushed the garment off his shoulders and smoothed her hands over his bare flesh, stroking him.

"Mmmmm, you are one buff hombre," she murmured.

"Hombre?" he asked, raising his head to look at her.

Her eyes flashed in a smile.

"Studmuffin?" she suggested. She moved her palms over his shoulders, down his chest, purring. "Very nice."

To his horror, Calvin felt himself blushing. "I lift a lot of stuff at the store," he muttered, looking away.

"Awww." The kiss she placed on his hot cheek was gentle. "I love me a humble sex slave."

That got his attention. "Sex slave?" he asked. *Love?*

She waggled her eyebrows at him.

"We'll see about that." He grabbed June around her waist and, as she squealed with laughter, carried her to the bed behind the Japanese screen.

He tossed her lightly onto the mattress and jumped on after her, crawling over her until he could look into her eyes. He gave her an Eskimo kiss, rubbing his nose against hers, and then a real one, taking her mouth with a passion that surprised even him. Now that his self-imposed restraint had been lifted, he couldn't seem to get enough of her.

"Calvin," she breathed and arched into his body. Her hands slid up his back under the shirt, fingers caressing the dip of his spine, the bit of extra flesh around his middle. Her legs tangled with his, and her feet, still in those sexy shoes, glided up and down his calves. "Calvin."

He pulled away, ran his mouth over her cheek, and then stood. He needed to be naked about five minutes ago.

June watched avidly as he stripped off his open shirt and threw it across the room. She didn't move from the bed; just laid there with her hair spread on the pillow like a dark cloud. She met his eyes and smiled, and let the leg closest to him splay wide, keeping the other bent at the knee, the tall spike of her heel digging into the comforter.

The position hiked the sexy red dress even higher up her thighs. Calvin drew in a sharp breath at the sight.

"God," he groaned.

"Lose your train of thought?" she asked in a low voice.

He realized he was standing stock-still, frozen in the act of unbuckling his belt, but her mischievous smile catapulted him into action. He whipped his belt off so quickly, he almost gave himself a friction burn. Shoes, socks, pants, and underwear quickly followed. Then Calvin was standing naked in front of June for the first time in fifteen years.

He briefly felt insecure about her reaction to his older body, but the thought was quickly washed away by the heat in her expression. Her gaze lingered on his erection bouncing high in front of him.

"Well, hello there," she murmured, laughing, and looked up into his face. "Why don't you bring that bad boy over here so we can get better acquainted?"

Calvin sat next to her on the bed and ran his hand up the calf of her propped leg, then over her knee and thigh. He toyed with the lacy hem of her stockings, with those sinful, red garters.

"I really like these."

June didn't answer. Her breath was coming in short, fast bursts, making her breasts rise and fall under the skimpy bodice of the dress.

He moved his hand higher still, under what passed for the skirt of her dress. June's eyes drifted shut. She had her hands in loose fists at her face, and he watched her suck on the knuckle of her forefinger, as if she needed to be tasting something.

His hard-on gave a jerk at the sight—he knew exactly where he wanted her mouth to be.

"God almighty," he whispered when he reached his destination and felt the tiny, damp triangle of fabric she was wearing. "A thong. You are fucking killing me, woman."

She moaned as he slipped a finger under the scrap of underwear to toy with her. Her back arched, breasts thrusting skyward.

"Calvin," she groaned, and moisture flooded over his hand.

He needed to feel her without the boundaries of her clothing. Helping her to her feet, he pulled the dress over her head, then stood back and just looked at her. Red lace bra, thong, garters, and stockings. *Gorgeous.*

"Christ, you're beautiful, June," he breathed and pulled her against him, ravenous for her. He took her mouth, tasting the flavor of her, so hot and spicy. *His June.*

Still kissing her, he unhooked the slip of a bra and let the mounds of her breasts free. They were heavier than he remembered but just as perfect. He filled his hands with them, pressing, massaging, and then he pulled at her nipples until she broke away from the kiss to cry out with pleasure.

He nudged her back on the bed and latched his mouth on one of those nipples, rolling it between his tongue and teeth, sucking, as she twisted beneath him. Her breasts had always been sensitive.

She scrabbled at his shoulders and tried to push him back so she could be on top, but he wouldn't let her. Instead, he kept the position of power as he feasted on her.

When he settled his body between her thighs, she wrapped her legs around him, and he felt the silk of the stockings against his skin, the sharpness of her heels, the wetness of her core rubbing against him as she thrashed on the bed. Finally, he couldn't wait anymore. It had been too long. He wanted it too much.

Calvin forced himself back, and pulled her thong down her long legs, working it off her shoes and throwing it over his shoulder.

"Thanks for not trying to rip it off," she gasped.

He grinned at her. "I know better than that. Nylon's strong."

"Advantage of sleeping with a hardware man," she laughed, and moaned when he ran his hands back up her legs. "No wedgies."

He was angry at the thought of other men trying to rip off her thong, but put it aside.

"Maybe you'll come up with some other advantages by the time we're done."

He got off the bed and found his pants, dug for the condom he'd been carrying in his wallet. Ripping the packet open with his teeth, he worked quickly to sheath himself, then turned back to June and stopped, transfixed.

She was flushed and damp, stunning in the stockings and shoes she still wore, the triangle of dark hair at the apex of her thighs framed perfectly by the red garters. She stretched and writhed in a sinuous motion that almost made him come on the spot.

"Get over here," she demanded.

He obeyed.

Settling beside her, he kissed her again, with so much force that their teeth clashed. He played with her breast with one hand while the other smoothed down to where the moisture from her desire almost flooded the bed.

He pressed a finger inside her, then two, stretching her, opening her, rubbing his thumb against the nub that was the center of her sensations.

"Calvin!" she broke away from his mouth. "Now!"

Unable to hold back any longer, he positioned himself and pushed the head of his erection into her body.

They both moaned.

She was so hot, and wet, and tight. And *June*.

Calvin drove forward slowly until he was fully seated inside her, waited until she tried to force him to move. Then the leash he'd been holding over himself snapped like a rubber band.

He withdrew, thrust back, and was soon pounding into her so forcefully that he pushed her up against the headboard of the bed, rattling the frame against the wall. Hell, for all he knew the whole garage was shaking.

He had just enough presence of mind to keep kissing her, keep playing with her breasts, desperately trying to bring her along with him, because he knew he wasn't going to last long.

June scratched his back with her nails, wrapped her legs even more tightly around him. Her head was thrown back, her mouth open, her eyes closed. Then she tensed, arched, and screamed out her climax.

Letting go, he followed.

15

After her explosive orgasm, June dozed for a while, waking to find the summer sun finally setting outside the apartment window. Her body felt loose and limber, and she smiled to herself, enjoying the tickle of Calvin's chest hair against her back, basking in the fiery heat of his body as he spooned her, his arms wrapped around her waist, his mouth moist on her neck.

Okay, she was big enough to admit that he had rocked her world. And she couldn't wait for him to do it again. She squirmed just thinking about it.

"What's wrong?" he murmured, not moving.

"Nothing," she said and turned in his hold to face him. Burrowing her face against his shoulder, she inhaled his scent, intensified by the sweat of their lovemaking. "Not a goddamn thing." She started licking the salt off his skin.

Calvin hummed, held her closer, and she felt his body stirring.

"Pretty good recovery time for an old guy," she teased.

To her surprise, he didn't laugh, but actually stiffened and pulled away a little bit.

"Hey, where are you going?" she held onto his arms so he couldn't escape.

"I know I'm not the kid I used to be, but it was good, right?" he asked. She was startled to hear the thread of doubt in his voice.

"Are you kidding?" She leaned back to study him. The room's dim light softened the planes and angles of his face, darkening his eyes and hiding their expression. "Of course it was good. I practically shot through the roof."

He smiled, and she could see his confidence returning. Who knew he would need reassurance?

"What about you? Was it good for you, too?" she asked, only half joking.

Usually, she didn't really think about such things—she could tell whether or not a man was satisfied. But the last time Calvin had seen her naked, she had been twenty-three, and now she... wasn't.

"You're stunning, June," he said, running his hands down her back to cup her naked ass. It was only then she realized she was still wearing—well, *mostly* wearing—her garters and stockings, although she'd kicked off the shoes at some point. "Round and full and womanly. You've grown into yourself."

"You, too," she said, and let her hands wander over the breadth of his chest, the hardness of his biceps.

Yum. She'd always been a sucker for a well-put-together man, and Calvin was definitely that. He'd been whipcord lean back when they were younger, but now he'd matured into pure strength. And she was dying to get her mouth on him.

So, why was she waiting?

Dipping her head, she took a bite of his firm pectoral muscle, sharp enough to sting. He gasped, and just that quickly, his erection was hard and strong between them.

"June." He cradled her head in his hands, wordlessly encouraging her to keep going.

Obligingly, she licked the small wound, tormented his flat nipple until he was moving restlessly beneath her. Smiling against his skin, she continued down his body, taking her time, pausing to kiss here, suck there, until she was finally where she wanted to be.

She paused and looked at him. Then, slowly, she drew his length into her mouth. When she'd taken as much as she could, she swallowed around him.

"God!" He dug his fingers into her hair. She smiled again, then sucked and lathed him until, desperately, he pulled her off.

"Inside you," he growled. "Now."

June felt a moment of triumph, but since she was soaking wet with her own arousal, didn't take time to gloat.

Instead, she reached over him to her side table, got a condom out of the drawer, and covered him with it. Resisting his attempts to pull her under him, she straddled his lean hips, and took him into her body, lowering herself with agonizing care until her butt rested on his thighs.

They both shuddered at the sensation of him stretching her.

Calvin ran his hands up over her breasts, and she jerked at the feel of his callouses on her sensitive flesh. God, she *loved* his hands.

Unable to stay still, she started to move. Balanced against his chest, his heart pounding through her fingertips, she rode them both into oblivion.

Later—she didn't know how much later—she woke from sleep to hear the splash of water as Calvin cleaned himself up in the bathroom. After another moment, he walked back to the bed and stood looking down at her.

It suddenly occurred to her that they'd forgotten to close the Venetian blinds, and the sun had set. Since he was still naked, and hadn't bothered to turn off the bathroom light, Ms. Gregory might be getting quite a show.

She got up quickly and shut the blinds, looking back at the sound of his deep chuckle.

"I don't think she's there," he said. "Or else she's asleep. Her house is dark."

"Still." June felt awkward, now that they were both awake, and the passion had been banked for the moment.

Calvin leaned against the bed, his smile fading into a somber expression.

"Do you want me to go?" he asked.

"Do you have to go?" she countered.

He sighed. "I probably should. I have to be up early tomorrow to open the store."

"You could, you know, sleep here," she suggested casually and tried to ignore the fact that she never let her dates sleep over. Never.

For whatever reason, she was reluctant to see him go. But that was okay, right? He was a hell of a lover. Might as well keep him around.

He raised his eyebrows. "Stay all night? People might talk."

"People *will* talk," she corrected, because there was no "maybe" about it. She considered him. "Do you care?" Was he going to run away now that he'd gotten laid?

In answer, he walked over to his clothes and pulled his cell phone out of the pocket of his khakis. Without taking his eyes off her, he threw the pants carelessly back on the floor and dialed the phone, holding it to his ear.

"Dad?" he said after a minute. "Sorry it's late...yeah, I know. I wanted to see if you would be okay alone if I stayed out tonight. Yes, all night." He listened, his face hardening. "Yes, of course I'll still open the store." He was silent again. "See you tomorrow." He clicked off and, still looking at her, tilted his head. "All right?"

June swallowed. "All right."

Her stomach chose that moment to growl, long and low, like she had a rabid wolf living in her gut. They both laughed.

"I think that's a cue for food," Calvin said, putting his phone on her nightstand.

"First, I'm going to get out of these stockings and take a shower."

"I think you should live in those stockings." His dark eyes glinted as they moved over her. "But go ahead and take a shower." He paused. "Need any help?"

It was pretty evident his interest was stirring again. June shook her head, a little dazed.

"For heaven's sake, man. Are you thirty-nine or nineteen?" she asked. "You should be down for the count by now."

"What can I say? I have a lot of pent-up demand." He walked to her, eyes lowered demurely. "Don't worry, ma'am. I'm sure I'll be able to make myself useful."

June crossed her arms and stroked her chin with her fingers. "Thinking outside the box?"

His smile was evil. "Maybe outside. Maybe in."

She pulled him with her to the bathroom.

Although Calvin was indeed still interested, he was forced to admit that he'd reached his limits for the time being. However, that didn't stop him from making sure June had a very thorough shower. Afterward, she told him that she would certainly give him a good performance review.

"Thank you, ma'am," he said.

Since June had fully intended on staying in for the evening, she'd stocked enough food to feed a starving army. They sat together at her tiny kitchen table, enthusiastically devouring thick sandwiches until, hunger satisfied, June sat back, relaxed and replete in her thick robe, her wet hair still bundled in a towel.

She watched Calvin start on his third sandwich, enjoying

the sight of him dressed only in boxers, droplets of water from the shower gleaming on his chest.

"Everything okay at home?' she asked, suddenly remembering his expression when he'd talked to his father.

He grimaced, chewed, and swallowed with a mighty effort, then took a long drink of water.

"Fine," he said. "Mom had been kind of agitated, but Dad's calmed her down. Hopefully she'll stay that way, so they can both get some sleep."

"Does she wander around the house at night?" June remembered reading somewhere that Alzheimer's patients could get restless.

"Sometimes. We have to watch her."

"Your life must have been a lot different when you were in the city. I know you had the divorce and all that drama, but coming back, being tied down to your parents like this... Well, it must be hard."

He shrugged. "Like I told you, I wanted to come home. Yeah, I get a little pissed off every once in a while. But, trust me, I'd rather be here. Especially now." He grinned at her and finished the last of his sandwich.

June toyed with the rim of her water glass as she looked at him.

"If I asked you why you and Kimberly got divorced," she said, bringing up the subject that had been rolling around in the back of her mind since the night her car had broken down, "would you tell me?"

He might not think it was any of her business, but she was curious. He had said he'd screwed up when he'd married Kimberly. Fine. If he felt that way, why the hell had he stayed with the woman for almost fourteen years? There was commitment, and there was stupid. Calvin wasn't a stupid man, so he'd had a reason to stay. And a reason to finally leave.

He raised his eyebrows in surprise and swallowed before

shoving the empty plate aside.

"You know why. I didn't love her," he said cautiously.

"Still. You stayed with her for a long time before you made your move."

He clasped his hands on the table in front of him, his eyes on her face.

"Okay. After I'd been with Kimberly for a few years, I stayed mostly because I was already married to her." He jerked a shoulder in a shrug. "So, she didn't want kids. So, she wanted to be a society queen. So what? What did I care? We were comfortable, so might as well make the best of it, right? And, like I said, I felt that I had an obligation to try and work things out."

"Then what changed? Or was she the one to ask for the divorce?"

"No, it was my idea." He sighed and looked away. "About a year and a half ago, I saw you on one of my trips home." He glanced at her again, eyes bleak. "I'd been going out of my way to avoid seeing you when I was here, but that time I zigged when I should have zagged. And there you were. With Pat."

June frowned. "I don't remember that. I would have remembered running into you." *Because it would have knocked her flat.*

"I ducked into a doorway like a moron. You kissed him," he added softly. "Right there in the middle of Main Street. And then you laughed with him, smiled at him, held him."

He got up and paced restlessly to the window, lifting one of the venetian blind slats with a finger to look out before turning back. "I saw you, and it was like I'd been slammed to the ground." He shook his head. "No, that's not right. It was like I suddenly woke up. I knew that I couldn't do it anymore. I just couldn't keep living the lie."

"Calvin—"

"I went home and told Kimberly I wanted a divorce. At the time, I never expected I'd move back here, that I'd see you again, that we'd...well. I only knew I couldn't live with her the way I'd been, pretending everything was okay. I had to get out." He came to stand beside her. "You know the rest."

June wasn't sure she did, but when he held out his hand, she let him lead her back to the bed.

The next morning, Calvin had to leave early to open the hardware store. June saw him off, standing on the landing, waving as the big, red truck rumbled down the driveway. When she went back into the apartment, her telephone was ringing before she'd finished closing and locking the door.

She checked the caller ID and rolled her eyes heavenward before answering.

"Hello, Ms. Gregory."

"If you two keep up this kind of thing, you might want to be more careful about your blinds," the older woman cackled.

June walked to her window and frowned at the white house next door. "How much did you see?"

"Let's just say I understand why you've been mooning over Calvin Hardy all these years." Ms. Gregory let out an exaggerated sigh. "Lordy, but that man is all kinds of fine."

June winced when she thought about Calvin's likely reaction to news of their voyeur.

"Your house was dark," she challenged. "You weren't even home."

"You'd like to believe that, wouldn't you?" Ms. Gregory cackled again and hung up.

"Great." June sighed, but couldn't work up the energy to get too irritated.

Putting the phone back on the table, she laid down on her bed, stretching and purring as she remembered the night before. She turned, buried her face in the pillows, and breathed in the scent of Calvin.

Oh, yeah. Ms. Gregory was right. That man was *all* kinds of fine.

16

June slept like the dead, ate like a horse, and took a long, hot bubble bath in her minuscule bathtub before heading to work at the Country Time later that afternoon. Hannah was already in the kitchen when she got there, swearing as she cleaned the fryer.

The younger woman straightened and gawked when June sang out a cheery "hello" as she breezed by.

"Who are you?" Hannah yelled after her.

June laughed, in too good a mood to care what people thought. Her hips were loose, her body lubed and tended. She figured she was probably glowing like a freaking lightning bug.

Humming, she threw her purse in Hannah's office and went to the storage closet for cleaning supplies.

Calvin had called her when he'd taken a lunch break around one, and she shivered remembering his deep voice on the phone. He hadn't been able to leave the store to come see her, but he'd promised to stop by the bar tonight after the bowling leagues were done. Maybe, if everything was okay with his parents, she'd be able to convince him to come home with her again.

She smiled, taking cleaning spray and a rag out to the taproom. Indications were, she wouldn't get much of an argument. She found herself humming once more, as she started wiping down the old wooden tables.

It had been good between them. More than good—it had been spectacular. True, that meant the whole exorcising demons thing wasn't going precisely according to plan. But how could she have known her memories *hadn't* exaggerated the way they were together? If anything, she'd forgotten a few details along the way.

She stopped humming and frowned at the square table she'd been buffing to a shine.

It was okay as long as she was careful about how much she hoped for or expected. And that would definitely be easier said than done.

She wondered if the decision to enjoy Calvin had been a huge mistake.

"What's wrong?"

June jumped about a foot at the sound of Hannah's voice coming from the end of the bar. Turning, she glared, wondering how long the jerk had been standing there watching her.

"Nothing's wrong."

Not in the least intimidated, Hannah leaned her hip against a bar stool.

"I beg to differ. First, you've been humming since you got here. Humming 'Happy' by the way, which is disturbing."

June cursed. Had she really been humming "Happy"? That was embarrassing.

"But now here you are, glaring at that poor, defenseless table like you want to pluck out its wooden liver." Hannah grinned. "I figured you'd be in a good mood today since I'm pretty sure you got lucky last night."

June blushed. *Blushed!*

"What's it to you?" she growled.

Hannah hooted with laughter and pumped both fists in the air.

"I knew it!" she crowed. "I knew Calvin would finally cave when you pulled out the big guns. You wore the red dress, didn't you?"

June crossed her arms and scowled at the girl she loved like a little sister.

"The man was toast." Hannah laughed, loud and long. "Toast, I tell you!"

"So maybe Calvin spent the night," June said, sounding defensive even to her own ears. "So what? It's not a crime."

Hannah sobered abruptly.

"He stayed *all* night? Even after you were...um... finished?"

June jerked a shoulder, mentally cursing when she realized the other woman knew she never let anyone stay overnight.

"Maybe."

Hannah came to stand next to her, all traces of humor gone, her hazel eyes serious.

"Just promise you won't let him hurt you this time."

As if I had a choice the last time. "Please," June scoffed. "He won't hurt me."

"I remember, you know," Hannah reminded her softly. "I saw what happened. I was only a kid, but I understood enough to get how bad it was."

"Yeah, well." June looked away and wiped absently at the table with her rag. "Maybe it was partially my fault, too. Maybe I expected more of him than he was willing to give. No," she amended, "more than he was *ready* to give." She spoke slowly as she worked it out in her mind. "I didn't let myself see what was going on."

They'd both been so young. So sure of themselves and where they were going. So ready to take on the world.

"You cried," Hannah said, jaw set in a militant line.

She certainly had. And if it hadn't been for fourteen-year-old Hannah, with her sad eyes and shy smile, she might have gone down a path she would have regretted.

But the young girl had shown her that there was someone in the world who looked up to her. Needed her. And June had eventually managed to pull herself together.

"I won't let it happen this time," she promised, and meant it. "I've changed, and I think maybe Calvin has, too. For now, he's interested, I'm interested, and we're actually getting to know each other again." She shrugged and made herself smile. "I'll just...see where it goes."

The kitchen door pushed open.

June stiffened in surprise as Eva Hardy shuffled into the taproom, large purse clutched in front of her thin chest.

"Hello," Hannah said, her voice polite. "Can we help you?"

"Oh, yes." Eva's face lit up with a smile. "I'm looking for Freddie. Is he here?"

Freddie? June glanced at Hannah, and the younger woman raised her eyebrows.

"Do you mean Fred Frederickson?" she asked Eva. "My father?"

"Your father?" Eva's eyes shadowed with confusion before brightening. "That's right. He has a daughter." Confusion again. "But she's only fourteen. You're not fourteen."

"No." Hannah looked helplessly at June.

June put down her cleaning rag and walked around the table to be closer to Eva.

"Can you tell us why you need to see Fred?" she asked, trying to be gentle with the older woman. This was the second time Calvin's mother had come to the Country Time looking for Fred. There had to be a reason.

"He told me to meet him here." Eva's dark eyes sparkled, and for a moment she was beautiful. "It's a secret."

Uh oh. June was very much afraid that the suspicions she'd had the first time Eva had come wandering into the bar might actually turn out to be true.

"Fred's not here," she said carefully. "He had to go…out."

"Oh." Eva's mouth pursed with disappointment. "But we were supposed to—" She broke off and put her fingers over her lips. "Secret," she whispered.

"Right." June thought quickly. "Should I call someone for you? Maybe your son?" If Eva knew Fred had a daughter, she should remember she had a son, right?

"Calvin?" Eva focused on June's face, her expression suddenly sharp and cutting. "I know you," she said abruptly. "You're dating my boy."

"I am?" June said, not sure what the woman was thinking.

"Stay away from him," Eva snarled, baring her teeth. "Whore!"

June sucked in a breath at the unexpected attack.

"What's your problem?" she demanded, asking what she'd always wanted to know. "What the hell did I ever do to you?"

"Fred wants *you* now," Eva growled, taking a step toward her, and holding her purse as if she would use it as a weapon.

June stared at her. Never, not in a million years, had she thought that this was the reason Calvin's mother didn't like her. Her background, her ethnicity, her supposed character, yes, but never because of Fred.

"There's nothing going on between us," she said. "There never was."

"It doesn't matter." Eva took another tottery step forward, her face a twisted mask under the bob of white hair. "I've seen him look at you. He watches you all the time. He watches you walk, and he smiles *that* smile."

June held her ground as the older woman approached. "I was never with him," she told Eva. "Never. You don't have to hate me."

"That's not what he says." Eva lost her balance, and Hannah

jumped to catch her before she fell. "That's not what he's telling everyone."

"Why don't—" June moved to take Eva's other arm, but the woman jerked back and clung to a chair.

"No!" She almost screamed the word. "Don't you touch me!"

They all jumped when there was sudden, loud pounding on the Country Time's front door. Hannah, eyes wide and face pale, shot June a look, then went to answer it. June wasn't entirely surprised when Calvin and his father burst into the room, their eyes wild.

"Eva!" Ronald ran to his wife. He was a big man, like his son, hair thick and white, face lined, shoulders broad under his polo shirt; although he was definitely thinner than he should have been.

"Fred?" She blinked at him.

Pain flashed across Ronald's face, and he took Eva's hand. "No," he said. "Come on home with me now. You need to rest and take your medicine."

"They told me you weren't here."

"They were right." Ronald swallowed. "Fred's not here."

She stared up at him for a moment, uncomprehendingly.

"Ronnie?"

Ronald closed his eyes briefly, then opened them again and looked down at her.

"Come on, Eva. Give me your keys. I'll drive you home now."

She studied him. "Okay." She rummaged in her purse, handed him a ring of keys, and slipped her hand into the crook of his arm before frowning at June.

"Have we met?" she asked politely.

"I'm June," June said, throat thick.

Eva regally inclined her head. "Nice to meet you." She looked up at her husband. "Let's go home."

Ronald nodded, smiled weakly at June and Hannah, then lead his wife through the taproom and out the door.

Calvin watched them go. His face was bone white under his tan, his expression lost and helpless, his hands hanging limply at his sides. June hurried over to him.

"I have to go," he told her, but didn't move. "Dad might need help getting her settled down." He ran his hands distractedly through his hair. "They came into the hardware store, and he and I were talking about something. We looked up, and she was gone. Then we saw their car was gone, too."

"It's okay." She gripped his thick bicep, fingers digging into the muscle as she tried to ground him.

"She drove. God, June, she *drove*." Calvin's voice was agonized. "I didn't even know she still had keys. Dad said he didn't have the heart to take them away from her, and she's never alone. I didn't know...."

He swallowed hard, and when he looked at her, there were tears in his eyes. "She could have killed herself or someone else so easily."

"But she didn't." June put her free hand on his face, felt the roughness of his whiskers against her palm.

"The hardware store is on the other side of town. She would have had to—" he broke off and shuddered.

"Calvin." June embraced him, and he immediately wrapped himself around her, burying his face in her neck.

"When we realized she'd taken the car, he knew where she'd gone. He knew..." Calvin's voice was muffled against her skin, his arms iron bands around her body. She thought she might have bruises from how tightly he was holding her, but that was okay. She pulled him closer still.

"Did you know about her and Fred?" she asked him softly.

"No." He drew in a deep, unsteady breath, then raised his head to look down at her. His eyes were red-rimmed and moist, but he gave her a strained smile. "No wonder she didn't like you. She was jealous."

"She didn't need to be."

"I know."

Such a simple statement. *I know.*

"You'd better go," she said after a moment. "Your father needs you."

"Yes." He glanced toward the door where Ronald had led Eva, then back at her. "I'll talk to you later."

"Later," she agreed.

Calvin kissed her hard, set her away from him, and left. As soon as the door closed behind him, June felt the strength leave her legs. She dropped into the nearest chair, rubbing her hands over her face.

"Jesus."

Hannah pulled out the chair next to her and almost fell into it.

"My father...and...Mrs. Hardy?" She swallowed. "They were a...thing?"

June sighed. "Sure seems that way."

Hannah nodded and looked down at the table, picking at the varnished top with a fingernail.

"And he was after you, too?"

"Yes." June knew the girl loved her father. But she wouldn't lie to her.

"And there were others."

"Oh, I would expect so." Now that June thought about it, Margo Truelove had been a Country Time regular back in the day, and there'd been a few others she suspected might have been having fun with Fred.

Hannah was quiet for a long time. "I know he hurt a lot of people," she said at last.

June just nodded.

"My mother...if she'd lived, maybe she would have left him."

"Maybe she would have," June agreed. She didn't know why Hannah's mother had stayed with Fred as long as she had, but she suspected it was for the same reason June herself had hung around.

"She stayed for you," she told Hannah now. "Because she wanted to make sure you had what you needed. And if she'd left him, she would have taken you with her."

"You stayed for me, too." Hannah's eyes were wide and luminous, the tears she was obviously fighting making them shine. "He tried to force you to...have sex with him, didn't he?" she asked quietly.

"He never tried to force me." June reached over and put her hand on Hannah's. "He just made me an offer."

"And you said no." It wasn't a question.

"I said no," June agreed.

"And he started rumors."

June tightened her hold.

"There were rumors. I don't know if he started them or not. There was always gossip." She grimaced. "I was young, had a Hispanic last name, and came from Philadelphia. There was bound to be gossip."

"But Mrs. Hardy, she really was sleeping with him."

June shook her head. "It's hard to tell. She's sick. Maybe she wanted to have sex with him, and now she thinks she did. We don't know, Hannah."

Hannah nodded and glanced away. June took her chin in her fingers, bringing it back so their eyes met again.

"Your father was who he was," she said. "But he loved you."

That wasn't exactly a lie, but she was definitely shading the truth. Fred might have loved Hannah in his own way, but until he'd gotten sick, he hadn't bothered to show it much.

Once Hannah was old enough to run the place on her own,

June had fully expected him to dump the Country Time on her and head off into the sunset. He'd stuck around longer than she'd thought he would, and then the lung cancer had come. Everything had changed after that.

On the other hand, she'd been there, supporting Hannah at her father's bedside during his last days. She'd seen how Fred's eyes, filmed over with drugs and impending death, had latched onto the girl. He'd clung to her hand, his own so thin that it looked like a claw.

Yeah, he might have been a dick, but Fred had loved Hannah as much as he'd been capable of loving anyone besides himself.

Hannah sniffed and nodded. Sniffed again.

"I'm glad you stayed," she said.

Then she threw herself into June's arms, and they were both crying.

17

Calvin pulled his pickup into the driveway of his parents' house, turned off the engine, and sat staring at the old farmhouse where he'd grown up. The graceful sweep of the porch roof and the traditional white siding against the black shutters juxtaposed with the new ramp they'd put in to make it easier for his mother to get in and out.

Had she really been having an affair with Fred?

Numb, he got out of the truck and walked slowly up the porch steps and into the house. He found his father sitting in the kitchen, drinking, a bottle of bourbon open on the table in front of him.

Not speaking, Calvin went to a cabinet, got another glass, and poured himself a shot. He sat down and drank it all, feeling the burn of the alcohol.

"Where is she?" he asked.

Ronald sipped his drink, slowly but steadily.

"In bed. She was so tired she could hardly stand by the time I got her home."

Calvin nodded, turning his glass in his fingers, looking at it instead of his father.

"Was she bad last night?" he asked.

His dad sighed. "Well, she's definitely been more agitated since that aide told her the gossip going around about you and June, but I thought she was okay." He shook his head. "Then again, I never really know what she understands. She was with me when I talked to you on the phone so she might have realized you were out with June all night. Maybe that's what set her off." He took a long swallow of bourbon. "Your guess is as good as mine."

Calvin put his empty glass on the table. He couldn't feel guilty about this. June was going to be a part of his life if he had anything to say about it, so he'd just have to deal with whatever his mother's reaction might be.

"Was Mom having an affair with Fred?" he asked bluntly.

Ronald drew in a breath, but he answered the question.

"Yes. For years."

"And you knew?"

His father drank, the familiar map of lines on his face deepening to make him look old and sad. He was quiet for a long time, but Calvin waited him out.

"Fred and I were the same age," he said at last. "We used to be friends, hang out together. The first time I saw Eva, he and I had dropped in at a local dance to try and pick up some girls." He smiled slightly. "She was just sixteen, and so pretty it made my heart hurt looking at her. Fred and I were older, closer to twenty, but she was the only girl I noticed that night. She might as well have been the only person in the whole room, as far as I was concerned."

Calvin had heard some of this before. "You married her when she was eighteen."

"Yes, but she'd been dating Fred before that." His father's smile turned ironic. "Maybe she was the only person I saw that first night, but she didn't give me the time of day. She was totally infatuated with Fred. Not surprising. He was a handsome bastard."

He took a long drink. "They, um, dated for a while. Her parents found out what their daughter had been doing, and who she'd been doing it with, and broke it up. I guess you could say I took advantage of the fact that she was on the rebound. They liked me a lot better than him because I was a Hardy, and we were settled with the store and all. So, Eva and I got married."

"But she was still seeing Fred?" Calvin couldn't keep the shock out of his voice.

"No. Not right away. I'm pretty sure they didn't start up again until a few years after you were born." Ronald sighed.

"She'd had a bad miscarriage and had to have a hysterectomy. I was working all the time at the store, getting things sorted out because Grandpa and Grandma had moved to Florida. Your aunts and their families were already gone, so there wasn't anybody else here to do it. She'd been angry and depressed but then she started getting happier. I was just relieved she seemed to be coming out of it, to tell you the truth. She wasn't quite as nasty." His mouth tightened.

"I didn't find out she'd turned to Fred for...comfort until later. One of the contractors saw them at a motel out on the interstate and told me."

"I'm sorry, Dad." Calvin didn't know what else to say. He was stunned.

His father wasn't looking at him. He was staring into his glass as if it held all the secrets of the past.

"I used to hate those fucking bowling leagues," he murmured. "She insisted we join. Good for business, she said. But she really wanted to be in a league so she'd have an excuse to sit all night at the Country Time after they were done and talk to Fred."

"Why did you stay with her?" Calvin asked. "Why did you

put up with it?" He didn't understand. His father wasn't a weak person—far from it. Why had he stood meekly by and let all this happen? Hell, by the end of their marriage, he and Kimberly had been nothing more than glorified roommates, but he didn't think he would have tolerated her having a long-term affair.

Ronald's mouth twisted, the expression in his brown eyes bleak. "I loved her. And I was certain she'd leave me if I told her I knew. Besides, my parents taught me that if you made your bed, you laid in it."

Calvin couldn't sit still any longer. He got to his feet and prowled restlessly around the kitchen.

"Okay, why did she stay with you then?"

"Fred had married Hannah's mom, and after Celia was gone, he didn't want anything permanent. Hell, he hadn't wanted Celia. And there was you. She loves you."

Jesus. Calvin gripped the edge of the countertop and lowered his head.

"What about June?" he asked. "You disapproved of her fifteen years ago because you thought she was with Fred, too, didn't you?"

He turned to see his father draw a hand through his white hair before letting it fall to the table.

"There was so much talk going around about her back then," he said. "I would hear it at the store, and when I came home your mother would tell me what people were saying about *that woman.*' That's what she always called June. *'That woman.*' I figured it made sense. She worked for him, right? So they were always together."

"But she wasn't having sex with him," Calvin pointed out.

Ronald shrugged helplessly. "I didn't know that then. I didn't find out the rumors weren't true until a couple of years later. It seemed logical, and I didn't want you ending up with a woman who would do that to you." His father looked at him, and there was fierce pride in his eyes. "You deserved more than that."

Calvin thought it through. "You didn't want history to repeat itself."

"I didn't."

"So you pushed me to drop her and leave."

"I encouraged it, yes."

Calvin barked out a laugh. "Right. Because ending up with Kimberly was such a *huge* improvement." He began to pace again. "I'm sure Mom was delighted to get me away from June's evil clutches."

His father shifted in his chair. "She wanted what was best for you."

"What was best in her opinion." His mother had been very clear. June Esperanza was not the right woman for her only child.

He could still remember his mom sitting at that kitchen table, looking at him with her large, dark eyes, telling him that everyone in town was talking about June and Fred. He hadn't believed the rumors, had known even in the midst of his stupidity that June wouldn't do that to him, but his mother's disapproval had weighed heavily on him.

"Do you think," Calvin said, "that Mom started the rumors about June?"

He'd always assumed Fred had started the gossip. It was something the asshole would have done to build himself up as a stud in front of his cronies. But now...

Calvin's dad shook his head and sipped his drink. "I don't think she started them. But she spread them. I believe she wanted June to leave town."

Calvin had to get out of there, get out of that house, and away from these people he felt like he barely knew.

"I have to go, Dad," he said.

His father's hand twitched, as if he wanted to reach out to him.

"I did finally confront your mother, you know. About the affair. After you had moved to Philadelphia, I told her I knew about Fred and that if she didn't end it altogether, I was going to tell you what she was doing, and divorce her without giving her any alimony."

Calvin studied him. "What did she do?" he asked.

His father chuckled harshly. "She went to Fred, of course. I gather he laughed at her when she suggested they take their relationship to the next level, so she came back. But she did break it off with him."

At what cost to you? Calvin wanted to ask the question, but didn't. He couldn't handle any more revelations.

"I really do have to go." He walked to the door, then hesitated. "Will you be okay here alone with her?"

Ronald nodded. "We're all right." He took a sip of his drink and looked at Calvin. "I didn't realize how much you cared about June," he said. "I'm sorry about that."

Calvin shook his head. "Good-bye, Dad."

He left father sitting at the kitchen table drinking bourbon and, he was sure, thinking about the woman upstairs who was still chasing another man, even after all these years. Even after the other man was dead.

Calvin sat in his truck for several minutes, staring out at the house, the gardens, the lush, green lawn. Then he started the engine and drove away.

He worked the rest of the day in something of a daze. When Austin came in for his shift, Calvin sent the kid home early and stayed to close the store himself. He couldn't face going back to his parents' house, couldn't face the bowling leagues his father had hated so much, and definitely couldn't go hang out at the Country Time and pretend everything was okay. He felt like the world he'd known had suddenly been turned upside down, and he was at a loss as to how to handle it.

He needed June.

After he had closed the store, he locked up and sat in his office doing paperwork for a while. Then he got in Big Red and drove around aimlessly until he realized he was on June's road.

It was still early; she wouldn't be home for another hour or so, but he found himself turning into her driveway and parking alongside the garage. He got out and sat on her bottom step.

The night was soft and dark, humidity hanging heavy in the air. Light from Ms. Gregory's neat, white house and the lamp over June's apartment door spilled out onto the gardens and gave the flowers a golden glow.

He'd only been sitting there a few minutes when Ms. Gregory's back door opened, and he saw the elderly librarian's straight form come down the steps, walking towards him.

"Why are you here?" she demanded when she got closer.

"I'm waiting for June."

She studied his face in the ambient light.

"Gonna be a while. Want to come in for coffee or something?" she asked.

"Not really, thanks." He liked Ms. Gregory, but he just wanted to be alone.

"Suit yourself." She didn't move. "You're not here to break up with her again, are you?" she demanded.

"What?" Calvin frowned. "No! Of course not."

Ms. Gregory nodded once. "Good. I'd hate to think you were that much of an idiot." She hesitated. "Girl's always had a thing for you, even after you left."

It was nice to hear, especially tonight. "I've always had a thing for her, too."

"Play your cards right and it could turn into something special." She looked at him with her bright, bird-like eyes. "That kind of thing doesn't happen all the time."

"I know."

She nodded again. "Close the blinds this time," she said. "I've had enough of a show."

Calvin stared at her. "What?"

She just cackled and left.

He dropped his head into his hands. Good God, could this day get any stranger?

The night settled around him again, crickets starting to chirp now that Ms. Gregory was gone. He rested his elbow on his knee and put his chin on his fist, looking out at the bird feeder, silent after tossing squirrels all day.

His mother had been involved in a long-term affair. His father had not only known, but he'd also put up with it for years. Because, he said, he loved her.

Calvin knew if he was married to June, and she had an affair—his muscles tightened—he would confront her about it as soon as he found out. He'd fight with her, keep her in bed for a month if he had to, anything to convince her that he was the only man she needed. She meant too much to him to simply ignore it.

If his mother really meant that much to his father, why hadn't his dad fought for her? And what about his mom? Had she been so desperate for Fred that she hadn't cared who she hurt?

Did he know his parents at all?

He sat, thinking about everything and nothing, watching the lightning bugs suspended in the air over the gardens, their little lights flashing off and on. Something rustled out in the underbrush. With his luck, it was Bigfoot. Or a bear.

Eventually, Ms. Gregory's first floor went dark, then the second floor lit up. He saw her look out at him from her bedroom window before she pointedly drew her blinds.

That made him both wince and smile.

Soon the second floor was dark, as well. Calvin sat on the step under the light from June's apartment. Waiting.

Every so often he heard a car or truck rumble past on the road, but it seemed to take forever for a pair of headlights to turn into the driveway. She was finally home.

Calvin didn't move. He stayed where he was, watching June's sedan make its way to the side of the garage and pull in next to Big Red. June turned off the engine, got out, and walked over to him with her loose, long-legged stride. She stopped in front of him, looking down.

"Hey," she said.

He tried to talk, but couldn't say anything. Instead, he wrapped his arms around her waist, nudged her between his thighs, and buried his face against her breast. The smell of her —so warm and alive under the clinging scents of beer and fried food—centered him.

She ran her fingers through his hair, cradling his head against her body. He sighed.

"You didn't come to the bar," she said after a while. "Bernie said you weren't at the leagues, either."

"No." He pulled back to look up at her. "You asked him?"

She shrugged. "He was bitching so loudly, everyone heard. They were a man short on the team, so they lost."

"Oh."

She smoothed her hands over his face.

"You didn't call."

He blinked at her. "Did you want me to call?"

June tugged his hair sharply. "Of course, you moron. I wanted to know how you were."

"I'm sorry." He was always saying that to her.

She tugged his hair again, harder this time.

"So, how are you?"

He rested his face back on her soft breast.

"Fine."

"Uh huh." June tilted his chin up and looked into his eyes for a long time. Whatever she saw there had her stepping back and taking his hand to pull him to his feet.

"Come on."

Unresisting, he followed her up the stairs to her apartment and stood on the landing while she unlocked the door. He let her lead him inside and watched her turn on the lights.

As she locked the door behind them, he suddenly remembered Ms. Gregory and went to pull down the window blinds. June saw what he was doing and laughed.

"Let me guess," she said. "You found out we had an audience last night."

He couldn't control the grimace.

"Prude." June pointed to her well-worn sofa under her wall of photographs. "Sit."

He did.

June sat next to him, wrapping her arms around his body, while he wrapped his around hers. He buried his face in her hair, content.

"Tell me," she said after a few moments. "What happened? Did you have to take your mother to the hospital?"

"No. She's at home." Calvin drew in a deep breath then, slowly—speaking into her hair at first, until he had to get up and pace around the small apartment—told her about his mother's affair with Fred, how his father had known, and how his parents had encouraged him to leave her.

June listened without interrupting, curled into the cushions of the sofa like a cat, her eyes never leaving his face, watching as he talked and paced.

"Your father was trying to protect you," she said, once he'd finally wound down.

Calvin shrugged. He didn't know how he was going to forgive either of his parents for what they'd done.

"What now?" she asked, reading his mind.

"I don't know." He walked over to the window and pulled back one of the blinds to look out into Ms. Gregory's dark, quiet yard, then let it fall again before turning to June. "My mother might have started those rumors about you," he said, leaning on the wall and crossing his arms. "If she didn't start them, she encouraged them."

"She was jealous." June pursed her lips. "I think she must have loved Fred, don't you? Wouldn't that have been hell, to be in love with Fred Frederickson and have to watch him with all of his other women? It must have driven her nuts. Then to have me there, certain I was doing it with Fred, only to find out I was dating her son, too?" She shook her head. "No wonder she hated me. I'm lucky she didn't come after me with a butter knife."

Calvin smiled and dropped beside her on the sofa. With a sigh, he leaned his head back against the rounded upholstery, closing his eyes.

"I don't know why Dad stayed, why he put up with it for all that time before he confronted her. He says it was because he loves her, but..."

"Letting someone walk all over you doesn't make it love," June concluded.

"No." He opened his eyes and looked at her. *Beautiful June.* "I walked all over you."

She rose onto her knees, facing him, and touched his cheek. "No. You maybe were careless. And I maybe wasn't paying enough attention. And we maybe didn't talk as much as we should have because we were too busy doing..." she bent over and kissed him, long and lingering, "...other things. But you didn't walk all over me. You didn't cheat on me and go behind my back with other women. I don't put up with that kind of shit."

He relaxed and grinned, leaning forward to kiss her again. "You would have punched me in the face."

"I would have punched you in the nuts," she corrected. "But I didn't have to."

"You'll never have to," he swore to her. "Never."

She smiled. "Because Hardy men keep their commitments."

"Yes." The phrase took on new meaning, knowing what he knew. Was that why his father had stayed? Was that what Calvin's life would have been like if he hadn't left Kimberly because he'd been dreaming of June?

"You're tired." She stood and pulled him off the sofa. "Come on to bed. You can decide what you want to do about your parents in the morning."

"Everything's different now," he murmured as he followed her around the Japanese screen and wearily started stripping off his clothes.

"Yeah, I know. That's the way it happens sometimes," she said sympathetically.

18

The following afternoon, Calvin worked out on the hardware store's small loading dock to sort some of the shipments they'd received earlier in the day for various contractors. He was thinking about June and wondering how many more hours it would be before he could see her again.

When the back door opened, and his father walked out to join him, he straightened in surprise. The elder Hardy hadn't been scheduled to come in that day, which had been something of a relief. Calvin had called the house that morning to say he'd be opening the store as planned, and their conversation had been almost painfully awkward.

"Hi." Ronald let the door swing shut behind him.

"Hi."

His father looked the same as he always did, big and tall in his customary polo shirt. Not a pretty man maybe, not like Fred had been, but solid. Dependable.

Or so Calvin had always thought.

"I saw Toby out front," Ronald said, wandering to the edge of the dock, hands in his pockets. "He told me you were out here."

"Yeah, I asked him to come in around eleven today." Although the other man usually worked in the evenings, Calvin just hadn't been in the mood to deal with the front of the store by himself and Austin had classes. Toby, a former roofing contractor who'd been scraping by ever since he'd fallen off a ladder and broken his pelvis pretty badly a couple of years ago, was glad to get the extra hours.

"I'm going to ask him if he wants to go full time," he added defiantly, not sure how the decision would go over. But enough with the procrastinating. If he wanted to have a life, they needed the help.

Somewhat to his surprise, his father just nodded. "Good. That's good." He stood looking across the parking lot at the building next door, booted feet planted on the concrete. Well, at least it didn't seem like they were going to have another tense scene.

"Where's Mom?" he asked, because his dad seemed to be alone. "Didn't you bring her with you?"

"No. I thought she should stay home today."

"Who's with her?" Calvin felt a pang of alarm. He might not know how to process all of the things he'd learned about Eva in the last twenty-four hours, but she was still his mother.

"Don't worry. Karen's there, and your mother seems less obstinate today than usual. Guess she's still tired. I asked Karen if she could stay all day, and the agency made arrangements. That's one of the things I wanted to talk to you about."

Hiking up his khakis, his father sat on the edge of the dock. After a moment, Calvin joined him, just like he used to when he was a kid and they'd take a break to eat the peanut butter and jelly sandwiches his mother always packed for them when he worked at the store.

The memory made him hurt deep inside.

Ronald was quiet, looking out over the parking lot.

"Since Karen was with your Mom, I took a long walk out in

the woods before I came over. Thought about a lot of things. Made a couple of decisions."

Calvin waited, not sure what was coming.

His father cleared his throat and looked at him. "I'm going to officially retire from the hardware store," he said. "It'll be yours to run as you see fit." He smiled faintly. "I still need an income, but we'll draw up some kind of a partnership giving you majority share. Or maybe I should just sign it over to you, in exchange for a monthly payment. We'll have to talk about what's best."

Calvin stared at him. This store had been his dad's life for forty years. How could he just walk away from it?

"Dad—"

"Stop it. This place is already more yours than mine, and that's the way it should be. You need to be free to run it without worrying about me. You gave up your whole life in Philadelphia to come back here."

Calvin thought about June's soft body wrapped around his as they lay in bed that morning. "I didn't give up anything."

Ronald shrugged and turned to gaze out over the parking lot again. "Doesn't matter," he said. "I've already called the lawyer."

"But what about you? What are you going to do?" Calvin asked, trying to comprehend what he was being told. His father loved the store, loved being there and talking to the people who came in. The social aspect was one of the reasons he'd tried to hang on, even as Eva's condition started to deteriorate.

"Oh, don't worry. I'll be in to bug you." Ronald smiled. "And I was thinking of maybe starting a handyman service. Seems like we don't have that kind of thing around here. What do you think about 'The Handy Hardy'?"

Calvin didn't know what to think about any of it. "What about Mom?"

His father leaned back on his hands. "I know she's getting

worse, but I hate to put her in a facility until I have to. When Karen came in today, I asked her if she'd be interested in working for us full time. She said she'd think about it."

Since Calvin suspected the matronly home health aide had a bit of a crush on his dad, he'd be surprised if she refused.

"See, I figure if you've got the whole store, you're not going to be home much. Besides, you'll probably move out soon, anyway," Ronald continued blithely. "If I don't have to worry about the hardware store, and I have someone to help care for your mother during the day, it should work out for a while."

Calvin's head spun. "And you can afford this?"

His father shrugged. "Honestly? I don't know. I've got savings, enough to go for a while. We'll have to be careful about making sure the store is safe, too. I want to be certain it's yours and doesn't get caught up in all this medical expense crap." He frowned thoughtfully. "I'll ask the attorney."

"I don't care—"

"That's what you say now." Ronald sighed and rubbed a hand over his bristly beard stubble. "Look, if your Mom goes into a facility, I'll probably lose almost everything because of the Medicaid requirements and all of the pay-downs and look-backs—bureaucratic bullshit. So why not keep her home as long as possible? Karen said she'd help me figure it out."

"Okay," Calvin said weakly, hands gripping the edge of the dock. "And you think I'm moving out, huh?"

His father looked at him soberly. "I figured you would. You want to be with June, right?"

"Yes." There wasn't any doubt about that. The only question was what June wanted.

"Then it's just a matter of time."

"Maybe."

They sat together in silence.

"I know you're not pleased with your mother or me at the moment," his father said eventually. "But we both love you."

"I love you too, Dad," Calvin said honestly.

Ronald nodded but wouldn't meet his eyes. Emotions made him uneasy.

"I also know you don't understand why I stuck by your mother for this long. Maybe I don't understand it myself. But I hope you know that I can't desert her now when she needs me the most."

"No." Calvin made up his mind. "And I'm still going to help you. I'm not going to desert her either."

His mother might be many things. She might be the heartless creature who'd cheated on his father for years, and the woman who'd spread rumors about June and told her son he needed to leave the person he loved. But she was also the one who'd made him peanut butter and jelly sandwiches when he'd come into the store, kissed his skinned knees, made an idiot of herself cheering him like crazy when he'd played football, and driven him to soccer games for years.

He could remember her teaching him to cook and dance, remember her laughing as they'd played killer croquet out in the backyard. He could remember the three of them—her, him, and his father—walking through the woods, while his old golden retriever, Hunter, splashed into the creek after a stick and came out again to shake water all over them.

He could see her dark eyes lit with laughter as she flung herself into his father's arms to make sure he got wet, too. He remembered the look on his dad's face, as if he'd entered heaven and was holding his own personal angel.

Maybe he did understand.

And the fact was, no matter what his parents had said or done, it had been his decision to leave town fifteen years ago.

"I'm not going to desert either of you," he said.

Ronald looked at him and nodded. "Thanks." His face creased into a grin. "We'll talk about my customer discount tomorrow."

The door behind them opened, and they turned to see Austin Grant standing there, looking nervous.

"Austin? What's up?" Calvin climbed to his feet. It was unusual for the kid to come into the store if he wasn't scheduled to work.

Austin shuffled.

"Um, hey. So I kind of have something to tell you, and I don't think you're gonna like it." His gaze darted beyond Calvin. "Maybe we should, like, talk privately."

"I have to go anyway." Ronald stood and clapped a hand on Calvin's shoulder. "I'll talk to you later, son."

Calvin met his father's eyes and saw it cost the older man something to leave him alone to deal with whatever this latest crisis might be. He smiled. Ronald Hardy might retire, but he was always going to care about what happened in his store.

"Later," he agreed, trying to show him he had no intention of cutting him out. Hell, if he was going to run this place on his own, he'd need as much advice as he could get.

His father nodded and left.

"Okay." Calvin crossed his arms once they were alone. "It's just you and me. What's going on?" A thought struck him, and he let his hands drop. "You're not quitting on me, are you?"

That would be all he needed. Austin had never closed, but he could do almost everything else. In fact, if his father wasn't going to be working at the store anymore, he should probably see if the kid could take more hours.

Austin gaped at him. "Are you kidding? This job is great."

Calvin relaxed. "So? What is it then?"

Austin went back to shuffling.

"I just...don't shoot the messenger, okay?"

He was going to kill him if he didn't spit it out soon. That thought must have been reflected in his expression because Austin hurried on.

"So, I didn't see my dad at breakfast today, cause I was late, but I had to call him to ask him something when I was on a break between classes."

"Okay." Calvin held on to his patience with both hands.

"He's in a bowling league, you know? Not yours, but one of the other ones."

"I know," Calvin said, not giving a shit.

"So, he told me you weren't at the leagues last night, and that Bernie Housemann guy was totally pissed off because your team was going up against the Hawks. He blames you because you guys lost, and you're one of the best bowlers. He figured your team would have won if you'd been there."

Calvin nodded. Bernie hated the Hawks because a couple of the members worked with Noah Chertok, June's contractor friend. Bernie thought the other man was stealing his business.

Bernie didn't quite get that the reason Noah had more business was because Bernie was a douche.

"So, Dad was at the afternoon leagues today. They bowl at lunch on Wednesdays, you know? And he said some of the guys were talking to Pat, just bullshitting and all. Bernie bowls then, too, on another team, and he brought up about you and your lady going to The Fallside for dinner and running out before you even got served."

Now Austin had Calvin's full attention. The gossip about that incident had died down after a couple of days. Why would Bernie try to stir it up again?

"He did?"

"Yeah. So anyway, apparently he was poking at Pat, saying how he guessed you and June had run off because you couldn't wait to hop into bed, and you were with June now, and didn't that make Pat angry to be so easily replaced, and stuff like that."

Goddamned Bernie.

"And Pat said, the hell with being replaced. He's not being replaced. He says June's never been with just one man anyway —she plays the field. He figures she's just jerking you around because she wants to get her own back for whatever happened between you guys years ago, and she'll leave you high and dry as soon as it suits her. Once she does, he fully expects her to try and come back to him. He said she's like a cat in heat, but sometimes she's worth the trouble."

The anger that burst through Calvin was blistering in its intensity. Hearing such things being said about his beautiful June made him shake with rage. He clenched his fists, breathing heavily, and Austin scampered back a few steps, holding up his hands as if to ward off a wild animal.

"I don't believe it! I didn't say it!" the younger man babbled quickly. "I mean, I did say it right now, but I'm telling you because she's your lady, you know? And I thought you'd want to know because now these bowling league guys heard Pat say that crap. My dad says he doesn't believe it because Pat was really angry at Bernie; he thought he was just whipping out his dick so Bernie would back off, you know? But some of the other guys who heard it think she's like that, and they're talking."

"Are they?" Calvin drawled. Austin winced.

"Yeah. So when Dad told me, I thought I should tell you. Toby told me you haven't been out front much today, but I figure people are going to start coming in as soon as they hear the gossip."

Calvin turned away from Austin to stare blindly out at the parking lot.

Damn them. Damn Bernie for poking at Pat. Bernie always liked to make trouble, always liked to watch something he'd said or done whirl through the gossip circuit. He got off on it. And damn fucking Pat Murphy for saying such things about June. Calvin didn't give a shit about himself; they could say what they liked about him. But June didn't deserve this.

"Are you okay?" Austin asked hesitantly.

Calvin turned and realized the boy was standing even further away now.

"I'm okay," he reassured him. "And yes, I did want to know."

"Okay." Austin visibly relaxed. "So, um, I'll just go now, all right? I have a class."

"Yeah. I'll see you tomorrow. And Austin? Thank you."

Austin grinned at him, and then shoved through the back door and was gone.

Calvin stood where he was.

He had to get to June. He had to make sure she was okay and let her know about the latest rumors, if she hadn't already heard them. He didn't want her to be taken off guard when the Country Time opened tonight.

Following Austin through the back door, he headed for the staff bathroom to wash up, then went to tell Toby he'd be gone for a while. As he came around a shelf, he saw Albert, Martin, Joe, and Harry standing at the counter, scowling at Toby on the other side. They were obviously furious. As a group, the old men turned to glare at him when he walked up to them.

"Have you heard the gossip about June?" Albert demanded before he could speak, skin drawn tight over his bony face. "Do you know what they're saying about her?"

"Yes," Calvin said shortly, his own anger exploding again.

"And what are you going to do about it?" Albert challenged. The four men stood with their arms crossed, looking like they would kick his ass if he didn't do what they thought he should.

"I'm on it," Calvin assured them. "First I'm going to go make sure June knows I don't believe what's being said. Then I'm going to go have a chat with Pat."

"You don't believe the talk?" Albert asked.

"Of course not." He stared at the other man. "Don't tell me you do?"

Albert rolled his eyes, but some of the rage seemed to leach out of his body.

"Of course I don't believe it, you idiot. And I'd be making sure she knew that, if I thought I was the one she needed to hear it from." He pointed at the door. "What are you still doing here? Get going. Once June finds out about this, she's gonna bust a blood vessel, and then she'll take an ax to Pat Murphy. Unless you want conjugal visits in jail, you'd better haul ass."

He was probably right. Calvin turned to Toby.

"I'm sorry," he said. "I have to be away a while."

Toby, blue eyes bright in his worn face, shook his head. "No big deal, boss. I've got it covered."

"We'll help him," Albert said. "Now, go."

Calvin went.

As he ran for Big Red, it occurred to him that the possibility the talk might be true had never even crossed his mind.

He believed in June.

He loved her.

Someday he'd make her believe in him, too.

He vaulted into the cab of the truck, started the engine, and peeled out of the parking lot.

19

June found herself doing something she'd sworn she'd never do. She was voluntarily cleaning the men's room when it wasn't her week to do it.

That's what Calvin had done to her. Instead of lounging in bed until a reasonable hour, enjoying the aftermath of the sweet lovemaking they'd indulged in the night before, she'd found herself up at the butt-crack of mid-morning, restless, wanting something to keep her mind off how sad he'd been, how his caresses had been as much about needing comfort as they'd been about passion.

It ripped her up to see him like that.

Even after she'd come in to work early that afternoon, she hadn't been able to settle. She'd wanted to call Calvin and find out how he was, but she didn't want to disturb him at the store.

So she cleaned.

June viciously scrubbed the commode in the last stall, thinking about Eva Hardy and her single-minded pursuit of Fred. Knowing Fred as she had, June didn't doubt that he'd thoroughly enjoyed it, too.

Was that love? If it was love, was it worth it? To be hurt, to cause so much pain to other people because you were fixated on one person? To remain fixated on that person even after he'd made it clear he wasn't on the same page?

June straightened, put the toilet brush back into its holder, and went to get a bucket and mop out of the storage closet. Returning to the restroom, she poured cleanser into the bucket, lifted it into a sink, and filled it with hot water, watching the steam rise into the air.

What about Ronald Hardy? He'd stuck with Eva, even after he'd found out she was obsessed with another man.

Was *that* love?

She turned off the tap and lowered the bucket to the floor. Dunking the mop in the sudsy water, she swabbed the vinyl tiles around the urinals, putting all of her restless energy into the motion.

If she and Calvin were together, and he started seeing someone else on the sly, and she found out about it, there was no way she'd just stand by and let it keep happening. She'd meant what she'd said the other day—she didn't put up with that kind of shit. She would kick him to the curb. After she'd chopped off his balls.

June paused, breathing a little heavily from the force of her exertion, and leaned on the mop.

But it was also true that Calvin would never do that to her. He'd never cheat on her, and he'd never go behind her back.

Look at what had happened fifteen years ago. Yes, it had taken a while for him to work himself up to talking to her about his decision to leave town. And yes, he'd let things fester longer than he should have, but he hadn't lied to her. He hadn't just wandered off or given her the illusion they'd had more than they did. He'd ended it before he'd gone; he hadn't left her hanging.

Calvin had told her what he'd thought was the truth, even

though it had been difficult. He'd hurt her, but he'd been honest.

The restroom door opened, and she turned to see Hannah step inside. The younger woman looked around, then whistled softly.

"Man, you should go through emotional drama more often," she said. "I've gotten more cleaning out of you in the past couple of weeks than I have in the past couple of years."

June shot her the finger.

Hannah laughed, then propped her shoulder on the door frame. "You okay?"

June shrugged and resumed her mopping. Since Hannah hadn't sought her out before now, she figured she'd been giving her some space to brood. The kid knew her pretty damned well.

"I'm all right," she said.

"Sure."

"Calvin's the one who had a ton of crap dumped on his head yesterday, not me."

"Right." Hannah didn't move, just watched her work. "And the fact that his mother might have spread some nasty rumors about you years ago doesn't matter to you at all."

So she'd figured out where some of that gossip might have come from. Well, the girl had always been smart. June stopped to lean on the mop again.

"No. It's done. Besides, Calvin swore he never believed what people were saying. He had other reasons for leaving town."

"Okay." Hannah studied her. "He's important to you. Calvin." She held up a hand when June started to protest. "Oh, please. If he wasn't, you wouldn't care what he thought."

June cursed but broke off when there was a sudden loud banging at the front door.

"What the hell? We don't open for another half hour." Hannah strode off to answer the summons.

June stood the mop up against a wall and followed her. She walked into the taproom and saw that Deacon, who was behind the bar getting ready for his shift, had stopped what he was doing and was heading for the big, oak double doors.

Hannah waved him back when she went past, then paused at the entry as the person knocked again, the sound echoing in the empty room. She looked out through a stained glass panel, then blinked, turned the lock, and opened one of the doors.

"Ms. Gregory?" she asked. "It's early. What are you doing here?"

The elderly librarian, dressed in one of the neat suits she wore when she was working, marched in and turned her bright, black eyes on Hannah and Deacon.

"I need to speak to June," she said, her thin mouth held in a straight line. "Alone, if you please."

Hannah looked at June.

June shrugged, wondering what the hell was going on. "Fine with me. Can we use your office?"

"Sure."

June led Ms. Gregory down the short hallway to Hannah's tiny space. After they'd crammed themselves into the room, she closed the door behind them and turned to the older woman.

"Okay, so we're alone. What's up?" She tried to think of anything she might have done to piss off her landlady in the recent past. Other than providing an impromptu peep show, she came up empty.

Ms. Gregory's face looked even sterner than normal. "I heard some disturbing talk at the library," she said abruptly. "When Milo Grant was in earlier, he had a phone call from his son. Since he was in the periodical nook, and didn't do me the courtesy of taking his call outside, I overheard what he was saying. Thank goodness nobody else was in at the time."

The periodical nook was right next to the check-out counter

and Ms. Gregory's desk, so June figured she wouldn't have had to strain very hard to eavesdrop.

"I thought you didn't allow cell phones in the library," she said. And what did any of this have to do with her?

Ms. Gregory waved her hand irritably. "Normally I don't, but Milo is an insurance inspector. I'm going to ask him to help me look into Claude Beecher's operation, so I've been cutting him some slack."

June tensed. "Claude? Ms. Gregory, what are you doing?"

The older woman adjusted the lapel of her suit. "As soon as Albert told me all of the issues you've been having with your car, and what Claude's response has been, I decided that *The Hardy Falls Gazette* should investigate."

June was appalled. It was true that Ms. Gregory was dedicated to her online newspaper, and she'd enlisted help from some of the journalism students at the local university, but so far the biggest story they'd covered had been a fist fight that had broken out at the council meeting a few months ago.

"I'm not sure that's a good idea," she said, "Claude might be dealing with some very bad people—"

"Which is why we need to look into it. It's a matter of community safety. Now shut up and listen to me," Ms. Gregory snapped. "Apparently there was quite a lot of talk going around about you at the noon bowling league today."

June stared at her, Claude all but forgotten.

"About me?" she asked carefully. "What do you mean, about me?"

Ms. Gregory watched her the way a coyote watches a rabbit.

"According to what I heard, Bernie Housemann was making fun of Pat. You know how Bernie is." She sniffed. "The man is an asshole."

"Yeah," June agreed.

"Anyway, he asked Pat how he liked being replaced, and Pat said he was not being replaced and that you were coming back to him. He said you are only with Calvin to get revenge for what happened before. He also seems to be of the opinion that it takes more than one man to satisfy you. I believe the term used was 'cat in heat.'"

June opened her mouth, but no words came out.

The librarian clasped her hands at her waist. "I realize you may think this is none of my business, but after I closed the library, I decided I should come over here to make sure you knew what was being said before the Country Time opens."

What the *hell*?

"But I'm not...I broke it off with Pat months ago. Christ, I broke up with him before Calvin even moved back to Hardy Falls." Except for that one unfortunate night she now knew had been a mistake of epic proportions.

Ms. Gregory's black eyes held no pity. "Pat does not seem to share your view of the situation."

"Pat's a jackass!" June wished there was enough room in the office to pace. "Of course I'm not going back to him."

"And are you trying to get revenge on Calvin?" Ms. Gregory persisted. "Is that why you're seeing him again? I know what happened when he left you, but he was young and stupid. I think he's a good man underneath it all, and I would hate to believe you were using him that way."

June wasn't sure what hurt most—hearing there were nasty, ugly rumors going around about her again, or hearing that Ms. Gregory believed them.

"Is that what you think of me?" she demanded hotly. "Do you honestly think I'd do that kind of a thing? That I could screw someone over that way?" Anger rose to the forefront, and she clenched her fists in an effort to control it. "You're right—it really isn't any of your business. Excuse me, but I have to go."

She tried to leave, but the other woman caught her arm in a hard grip.

"I thought so," Ms. Gregory said with satisfaction.

At a loss, June just stared at her.

Her landlady patted her arm before letting it go. "My dear, I believe you have a fairly large problem. Apparently, all of those idiots at the noon league heard what Pat said. Some won't believe him. Milo said he thought Pat was, and I quote, 'just whipping out his dick to show Bernie,' which isn't a pleasant image. But some of them will think it's true, and gossip travels fast in Hardy Falls."

Boy, did June know that. She thought about the speculative looks she'd get as soon as the Country Time opened and customers started coming in. The whispers. The smirks. Some of the men would try their luck, others would just watch her and leer. It had all happened before.

And what about Calvin? Had he heard these rumors? Did he believe them? How could he possibly trust her enough to know she would never act that way? This could destroy whatever was growing between them.

She'd known Pat was hurt when she broke up with him, but how could he say those things about her? And what would he say when she didn't come back to him? How would he explain it? What lies would he spread then?

Suddenly furious beyond all rational thought, she turned, jerked open the office door and stalked out. Over the roaring in her ears, she thought she heard Ms. Gregory call her name, but ignored her.

She wasn't quite sure what she was going to do, but it involved going over to the bowling alley and chopping Pat into tiny, muscle-bound pieces.

How dare he try to ruin her life? When this had happened fifteen years ago, she'd been young and stupid and in love, so she hadn't given a damn what people said. Then she'd been young and stupid and heartbroken, too tired to do much but let nature take its course until the worst of the talk died away.

She wasn't stupid anymore.

Whatever was growing between her and Calvin, it was too precious to mess around with a second time. This time, she would defend it.

Deacon called to her when she walked past the bar, but she ignored him, too, and shoved her way into the kitchen. Hannah, busy cutting potatoes for salad, looked up in surprise.

"I'm going out for a few minutes," June growled.

Hannah gaped at her. "Go out? What—"

June didn't hear the rest as she slammed out the door and headed across the parking lot to Murphy Lanes. A few minutes later, she stormed into the bowling alley with such force she scared some kids who were playing games at the machines in the lobby.

She saw Pat sitting in his usual place behind the shoe rental counter, looking like a gargoyle. He was perched on a tall stool, tight black T-shirt straining at the seams, and appeared surprised to see her, which just went to show how stupid he was. What had the man expected her to do when she heard what he'd said? Thank him for calling her a whore? Because that was pretty much what he'd done.

Paying no attention to the stares she was getting from people sitting at the bar waiting for evening leagues to start, she marched over to Pat, stopping when they were face to face with only the old laminate counter between them.

"What the hell?" she demanded, speaking loudly enough to be heard over the throbbing classic rock music and the sound of pins crashing in the lanes as bowlers warmed up.

"June," Pat said. He folded his arms over his massive chest and balanced the heel of a booted foot on the bottom rung of the stool. "What can I do for you?"

"What can you—?" She broke off, gripping the edge of the counter, unable to talk for a moment. "I heard you were busy spreading lies about me at the noon league," she said at last. "I'm here to tell you I want you to stop."

Pat glanced down toward the lanes, and June realized she couldn't hear the thunder of balls hitting pins anymore, just the continual pounding of the music. She didn't look but guessed they'd become the center of attention.

Good, she thought, feeling reckless. Bring it on. Pat had lied about her in front of the whole town, so let the whole town hear him justify his actions.

"I don't know what you're talking about," he said.

June wanted to jump over the counter and strangle him.

"Bullshit," she growled. "I heard exactly what you said. Did you think I wouldn't? Did you think I wouldn't come over and call you on it when I found out? You don't know me at all."

"I know you, June," he sneered. "I know *exactly* what you're like, and I'll say what I want in my own place."

She braced her hands on the laminate and leaned forward. "We are over, Pat," she said. "Finished. Do you get that? Is that sinking in? We've been over for months, but even if we weren't, we would be now that you've shown me exactly what you are. Stop talking about me. Stop trying to drag me through the mud just because I've moved on. I am done."

It was more than likely that she was the only one who saw the flash of pain in his eyes before it quickly morphed to anger. He stood, towering over her, and she took an involuntary step back.

"You can fool a lot of other people in this town, but you can't fool me." His smile was twisted, his attention entirely focused on her. "Yeah, I know you've decided to fuck Calvin Hardy again. So what? Maybe you just needed to scratch an itch or wanted to walk down memory lane. But I think you're doing it so you can screw with the bastard. I think you'll get as much out of him as you can, then dump him the way he dumped you."

"Oh, yeah?" she challenged.

"Yeah. You're using him," he snarled, shifting toward her,

"because that's what you do. Everyone knows how you used Fred, sleeping with the boss man to keep your worthless job. You used me. And you used all of the men in between." He shrugged, crossed his arms again. "Sure, I told the guys you'd probably come running back to me when you got tired of Hardy. But you know what? I wouldn't have you now even if you did."

June met his glare, refused to back down, even though the guilt raised its head again because in a way she *had* used him.

"You have no idea what's between Calvin and me," she told him quietly.

"Right." Pat laughed, a nasty sound. "You know the best part? He's just using you, too. Here he is stuck in this little nothing town, and you're pretty damned convenient. For all you know, he's going to embarrass you in front of everyone again and head back to Philly."

"No." A voice she hadn't expected to hear spoke from behind her. "He's not."

June whirled around and saw Calvin.

He was standing behind her with his feet planted, jeans low on his hips. If he'd had a revolver and side holster, he would have been the epitome of a lawman from the Wild West. He looked tough enough to tear Pat apart.

He looked like he wanted to do it, too.

Pat tensed. Someone stirred nearby, and June realized the bowlers weren't even pretending not to listen anymore. They'd deserted the lanes and the bar and were all standing around, staring.

"What are you doing here, Hardy?" Pat demanded, sounding very alpha dog.

Calvin ignored him and walked over to June.

"I stopped to see you," he said, speaking as if they were alone in the room. "Hannah told me you'd run out of the Country Time like it was on fire. Then Ms. Gregory said she'd let you know about the talk going around, so I figured you'd come here to break some heads."

"Smart man." She studied him, not quite sure how to read his expression. Was he angry with her? Did he believe Pat's lies? She could hear whispers, even over the music, and looked at the sea of interested faces surrounding them. "Maybe we should go somewhere else and talk."

"Yeah, why don't you both get out?" Pat said, leaving the shoe counter to stand across from them.

"No." Calvin's eyes didn't move from hers. "This town has been all up in our business for years. I want them to hear for themselves what we say. No room for doubt."

Her stomach knotted. What was he doing?

The pounding music suddenly flipped off, throwing the bowling alley into a hush that was actually painful. Behind the people crowded around them, the glass entry door opened, and Hannah strode in, followed by Ms. Gregory.

"What's going on?" Hannah demanded, pushing her way through the mob. "June? Are you okay?"

"I'm fine," June told her, although she wasn't entirely sure.

"Enjoy the show, Hannah." Pat crossed his arms, muscles bulging. "Calvin's decided he's going to air his dirty laundry in front of the whole town."

The observers tittered with excitement. Calvin looked directly at Pat for the first time.

"Not the whole town," he said. "And the laundry's not exactly dirty."

"Calvin," June warned, "don't do anything stupid." If he was going to get all up in her face because he thought the rumors were true, she'd be damned if he'd do it in front of everyone.

Calvin turned back to her, watching her in silence for a long moment. "And just what do you think I'm going to say?" he asked at last.

That was the question, wasn't it?

June tried to see behind his stoic mask. He seemed to be waiting for something.

It suddenly occurred to her that he might be waiting to see if she'd trust him.

Did she? Was that was the real question?

He'd told her he was sorry numerous times. He'd told her he never wanted to hurt her again. Did she believe him? Or was she fooling herself? Was he the kind of person who would tear into her in front of the whole town, knowing it would humiliate her?

No, of course not.

As she rejected the idea, the iron band that had been tightening around her chest eased abruptly, and she could breathe again.

No, of course Calvin wouldn't do that. If he had a problem with her, he would tell her. Alone. Not in front of everyone.

She put her hand on his arm, smoothing his skin, feeling the muscles tighten and relax beneath her fingertips.

"I'm waiting to find out what you're going to do to Pat, hotshot," she said, trying to sound cocky and arrogant. She didn't think she'd pulled it off, but Calvin's dark eyes lit up with relief.

Pat scowled. "He's not going to do anything except get the hell out of my place."

Calvin brought June's hand to his lips, pressing a warm kiss into her palm before lowering it to hold it against his side. Then he looked at Pat, and all traces of softness vanished.

"I hear you're pretty sure June is dicking me around because she wants to get back at me for what happened before," he said to the other man. "And you're also of the opinion that she's never faithful to one man. You seem to think she'll come back to you after she's done with me." He arched his eyebrows. "About right?"

Pat's face was flushed, but whether it was from anger or embarrassment, June could not say.

"Yeah, I think she's using you," he said belligerently. "I think you're an idiot to believe whatever line she sold you. I think she'll squeeze you dry and then dump you. And yeah, I think she'll try to come back to me after." His lips twisted. "As if that would work."

Calvin nodded. "Except the truth is, that's a pile of horse-shit. June Esperanza is the most loyal, most honest woman I've ever met. She would not try to hurt me for revenge. She would not cheat on me. She's with me because she wants to be with me. I hope she wants to be with me for a long, long time, because I'm looking for forever."

June stared at him, hardly able to take in what he was saying. *He believed her.*

Pat laughed, but his hands were fists under his armpits. "You really are an idiot."

Calvin shook his head. "No."

Pat studied him with some real sympathy. "You realize you're making an asshole out of yourself in front of the whole town, right?" He gestured to their audience. "Lots of people watching."

"I know." Calvin shrugged. "If she dumps me, everyone's going to be pointing at me and laughing. But I'm in it for the long haul. I'm going to try my hardest to convince her I deserve another chance."

June realized what he'd done. Not only had he made it clear to everyone that he trusted her, he'd also just handed her the power in their relationship. But she found that she didn't want all of it anymore.

"And I'm going to try to keep him from deciding he's had enough of me," she said. Calvin looked at her, and she smiled. "But that's up to him."

He kissed her, right there in front of the bowlers and Hannah and God and everyone. When he finally pulled back, June was breathless, people were talking, Ms. Gregory was scribbling in a notebook, Hannah was beaming as if she was a proud mama watching her baby go off to prom, and Pat was staring at the floor, his face set in rigid lines, jaw working.

"I think that's all, folks." Calvin tugged at her hand. "Come on."

"I'm taking a break," June told Hannah.

The girl rolled her eyes. "Well, *duh*."

June followed Calvin through the throng of interested viewers until he brought them to a halt in front of Bernie Housemann.

"I'm quitting your bowling league," Calvin told him. "Take my name off your roster."

"Now, Cal, listen—" Bernie started blustering.

"June is my…is mine. So you be careful how you talk about her from now on, get it?"

Bernie hiked up his pants and looked around at all of the people watching this scene play out. "Sure. No problem."

Calvin nodded and pulled June out of the bowling alley. He shook his head when she would have spoken.

"Not here," he said. "Let's find someplace private. We've given them enough to talk about."

She laughed shortly. "Are you kidding? We've given them enough gossip to last for weeks." Hell, if she knew Ms. Gregory, they'd probably be headliners in *The Hardy Falls Gazette* before the night was out.

They walked quickly to the Country Time, then around the building to the employee rest area out back, stopping beside the plastic Adirondack chairs.

June shifted from foot to foot, feeling nervous now that they were alone.

"I can't stay long," she said.

"Just a few minutes. We need to talk."

She pulled her hand away from his grasp.

"So talk," she demanded abruptly. "Did you mean what you said back there? All that stuff about wanting to be with me for a long time?"

Calvin cocked his head, and his hair flopped over his brow.

She folded her fingers into her palms to keep from reaching up to push it back.

"Don't you know?" he asked, his eyes dark in the early evening light.

"No, damn you." She moved to him, got right up in his personal space, and aligned her body with his. "How do you feel about me, Calvin?" she demanded. "How do you really feel? Tell me straight out."

For a moment, he simply looked at her. Then he rolled his eyes so hard she thought they might fall out of his head.

"Oh, for Christ's sake, woman! I just now crawled in front of the whole town for you," he yelled, jabbing a finger towards the bowling alley.

Remembering the pride and strength in his face, his voice, she smiled at his idea of "crawling."

"So?" she arched her eyebrows at him. "Maybe you're just letting yourself be ruled by guilt. We both know you're soft."

"Soft," he snarled. "I'm soft in the freaking head."

Before she could move away, he grabbed her and yanked her tight up against him, then kissed her, hot and hard and long. When he finally let go of her mouth, his eyes looked glassy. June was pretty sure hers did, too.

"I love you, you moron," he told her, emotion making his voice harsh. "I've loved you for years."

Everything inside her suddenly filled with light.

He loved her.

She cuddled close to him, wrapped herself around him like a vine. "You never said it. Not even the first time we dated."

"I was an arrogant prick the first time we dated. I didn't know what I was feeling until I'd tossed you away and was trying to be married to Kimberly."

She clutched him tighter and let her nails prick into his back. "Do me a favor and don't mention Kimberly right now."

"I won't mention her if you don't mention Pat or any of the other men you dated while I was gone."

"There were only a few others. Well, after the first year," she admitted honestly.

He held her more tightly, buried his face in her hair, and trailed his lips along her neck.

"I love you, June."

June drew in a deep breath and took the plunge.

"I love you back."

That's what the thing was between them. That's what it had always been. She loved Calvin. She'd loved him from the first moment she'd laid eyes on him, sitting all delicious and brooding at the Country Time's bar. She'd loved him even when he'd hurt her. And she'd loved him for all the years in between then and now.

Calvin kissed her again. It took them a long time to surface.

"I meant what I said at the bowling alley," he told her when he could talk. "I'm not leaving unless you kick me out."

She smoothed her hands over his face, enjoying the rasp of his whiskers against her palms. "Because you feel guilty?"

He frowned down at her. "Because I want to be with you. What part of 'I love you' didn't you understand?"

"Pretty much all of it," she admitted. "Nobody's ever really loved me before, except my grandmother. And Hannah."

"This is different."

She grinned. "It had better be."

He kissed her again.

"I do trust you, Calvin," she said after a while. "Knowing that you love me, knowing that I love you, it's a lot. It's everything."

"I still need to show you I'm serious." He frowned. "But it's okay. I'm on it."

She drew back, confused. "You're on it?"

"Sure." He grinned at her. "We'll follow the original plan.

We'll date. I'll take you out to breakfast, lunch, dinner, whatever. We'll cause all kinds of gossip when I make out with you at the movie theater. Ms. Gregory will splash our names all over *The Hardy Falls Gazette*."

"Old busybody," June grumbled.

"People will come into the hardware store and tease me and try to make me lose my cool."

June scowled and pushed further away. "They will?"

"Of course they will. It's fine, as long as nobody says anything bad about you."

"Calvin—"

"And I won't leave. I won't back off. I won't turn away." He stared down at her. "You got that, June? I'm not going anywhere. No matter what."

"What about your parents?" she asked quietly. "Your mother?"

He pulled her more tightly against him. "I hope you can forgive my mother, June. I don't know if she started the rumors about you and Fred or just repeated them because she was jealous. I know she went out of her way to break us up, to get you to leave town. But she's so sick, and my father needs me. I can't just—"

"Wait." She kissed him quickly so he'd be quiet. "I didn't mean you should leave them. They do need you. I just meant, what are you going to do if she disapproves of us? If it makes things harder?"

"I'll stay. I'll love you." He ran his hands up her arms and into her hair. "I'm not an arrogant prick anymore. I'm here."

Then he kissed her again.

EPILOGUE

A month after the showdown with Pat at the bowling alley, June was sitting at the bar in the Country Time rolling clean silverware into paper napkins and getting ready for another Wednesday night.

Catching herself humming, she saw Deacon grin at her from where he stood polishing glasses. She scowled at him, but she didn't really mind his teasing.

She'd been with Calvin for weeks now, and things just kept getting better between them. He'd taken her out on dates, including dinner at The Fallside for her thirty-eighth birthday. They'd actually managed to stay for the whole meal this time, although there'd been whispers when he'd kissed her in front of everyone.

June didn't care if they ever went back there anyway—she enjoyed it more when they went to the rib place, or the movies, or picnicked in the park on a sunny Sunday afternoon when neither of them had to work.

She especially loved the photograph she'd taken of Calvin the last time they'd been to the lake. He'd been lying on a blanket, head propped on his hand, the sun shining through the leaves of the nearby trees lighting his strong face. His expression when he'd looked at her...

She drew in a deep breath.

Realizing she'd just been sitting staring at the silverware, she started working again. Deacon chuckled.

"Go to hell," she told him without heat.

Ms. Gregory had published an opinion piece about the altercation at the bowling alley in *The Hardy Falls Gazette*, basically saying that people shouldn't believe everything they heard. June appreciated the effort but didn't think it would do much good. It was for sure Pat would never forgive her, but she was okay with that.

As far as she could tell, he'd stopped repeating the ugly talk, although gossip continued to float around town. She wished she hadn't hurt him, and could see how he might feel she'd led him on, but it was no excuse for what he'd said about her. Good thing she planned on staying out of his way from now on.

June just hoped the whole thing wouldn't cause more trouble for everyone in the future. She'd heard that Pat had gone on a real rant about the bowlers coming to the Country Time to eat and drink. In fact, according to the people she'd talked to, he was becoming almost obsessive about it.

Fortunately, he served crap food and only had one kind of beer, so it wasn't likely to be much of an issue. If the bowlers stopped coming to the Country Time, it could really impact Hannah's business.

Then there was the fact that Hannah's Uncle George seemed to be spending more and more time with Pat. Who knew what the two of them were talking about? Probably just Rotary business, but June had her doubts.

Still, those were all problems for another day. Right now she had better things to think about.

Smiling, she touched the silver necklace Calvin had given her that morning before he'd headed off to the store. It had a diamond heart fob engraved with, *"Never forget, you own my heart. Calvin"* on one side.

The gooey warmth that filled her made her sigh, then frown when Deacon laughed again. At least Hannah was busy in the kitchen banging pans around and cursing the fryer, or she'd never have heard the end of it.

Giving Deacon the finger, she grabbed the bottle of cleaning spray and a rag and went to wipe down the tables.

Calvin was still living at home, although they'd worked out a schedule with his father so that he could spend the night with her a couple times a week. Ronald had a nice home health aide named Karen coming in full time to help with Eva now, but Calvin didn't like leaving him alone with his mother every night. He'd asked June if she wanted to move in with him, and she'd told him she'd think about it.

She was sure it wouldn't work, though. They'd tried to have dinner with his parents one night, and it hadn't gone at all well. Eva had taken one look at June and started screaming, not stopping until June went outside.

Calvin had come out a few minutes later, full of apologies, telling her that he needed to take her home then come back to help his father. She'd understood. When he'd dropped her off at her apartment, she'd kissed him and told him to come back when he could.

A few hours later, she'd answered her door to his knock, taken one look at his face, and pulled him into her arms. He'd held her tightly enough to hurt, as if she was the anchor he needed to keep himself in place. Then he'd made love to her with an intensity he hadn't shown since their first night together.

She heard Hannah call out a greeting in the kitchen, and

wasn't surprised when the door opened, and Calvin came into the taproom.

He didn't hesitate, just walked up to her, wrapped her in a close embrace, and burrowed his face in her hair. She stroked his back and neck, trying to soothe him.

"How did it go?" she asked after a moment. Calvin and his father had taken his mother to a specialist, wanting to see if there was anything else they could do for her.

"Okay." He lifted his head to look at her. "The doctor was great. Mom was really upset about going, so he got to see what she's like at her worst. Thank God Karen came with us. She took Mom out to the waiting room after the examination so my father and I could talk to him without her being there."

"What did he say?" June asked, running her fingers through his short, thick hair.

Calvin sighed, his dark eyes shadowed. "He thinks we're okay for now with Karen coming in full time, but it might get to be more than we can handle. We'll have to see how it goes."

At some point, Eva was going to lose control of all her bodily functions. June hated to think about what that would mean for the proud woman and for the family who, in spite of everything, loved her.

Calvin ran his hands up her back and rested his chin on her shoulder for a moment. "Dad's more open to talking about a facility after the whole 'poop incident.'" He shuddered, and June shuddered, too.

One day, Eva had apparently forgotten what toilet paper was used for. Karen had gotten distracted by someone at the door, and since Ronald had been out at the time, Eva had used the opportunity to paint her poop all over everything.

It had taken Ronald, Karen, and Calvin hours to get it all off the walls, the sink, and the commode. June had bowed out of that one. She dealt with enough crap—hah—when it was her week for the Country Time restrooms.

"The doctor's going to adjust her medication again, so hopefully that will help," Calvin said. There was a slight crease between his eyebrows when he looked down at her. "You realize this means I won't be able to move out for a while. I can't desert my father now."

"I know." June cupped his cheek. She smiled at him with what she was sure was a stupid expression. "As long as you don't have to be there *every* night." Pulling his head down, she kissed him.

When they finally broke apart, neither of them was breathing very steadily.

"No," he said, and it took her a moment to remember what they'd been talking about.

Oh, right. His mother.

"We can find overnight help if we need it," Calvin continued. "Dad and I had a long talk after we got home. He understands I need to be with you."

"I hope he's okay about us," June said. She didn't want to come between Calvin and his parents. She never had.

Calvin kissed her again. "He's fine. But it wouldn't matter if he wasn't. Maybe I have to live with them for the moment, but you and me? We're a forever thing, June. Everyone had just better get used to the idea." He pulled her ponytail. "Including you."

June grinned so widely it made her face hurt.

A forever thing.

"I'm getting used to it," she said.

Yes, she was getting used to having him in her life. Used to being sure he wouldn't leave again.

Used to love.

She stood on her toes and kissed him. Hot and hard, deep and joyful.

Maybe the road hadn't always been smooth for them,

maybe there would still be rough patches in the future—but he was here, and he was hers. Just as much as she was his.

She was starting to believe it.

THE END

Turn the page to read an excerpt from

Handling Love
Welcome to Hardy Falls, Book 2

HANDLING LOVE
WELCOME TO HARDY FALLS, BOOK 2

Not everything in life can be business as usual...

Hannah Frederickson never, ever, gives up. She does whatever it takes to make sure her business, a popular local tavern, succeeds. The rest of her life can wait.

So when Hannah discovers that her uncle ran off with all of her money, nothing else should matter. Especially not a stupid and intense attraction to Deacon Black, her friend and the head bartender working at her bar.

After all, Deacon might be sexy as hell, but getting close to him just raises a whole new set of problems.

Handling Love is a cheekily humorous, charmingly sexy romance about two friends figuring out which way they want to go, in life and in love. When Hannah and Deacon finally understand what they should have known all along, "business as usual" flies right out the window.

~

Chapter One

"Go talk to my aunt," Hannah Frederickson said as she strode into the taproom of the Country Time Bar and Grill.

Her bartender, Deacon Black, looked up with a puzzled expression on his pleasantly rough face. He was standing behind the bar cleaning shot glasses in anticipation of the regular Wednesday night crowd. Well, maybe "crowd" was too optimistic, but they usually had a pretty good turnout when the bowling leagues were playing next door at Murphy Lanes.

"Huh?" he said.

"Go talk to my aunt," Hannah repeated. She walked behind the bar, slid past Deacon, and headed for the bottle of whiskey sitting on a nearby shelf.

"Now?" he asked, turning to watch her, obviously still confused. "We're going to open soon, and she lives across town."

"No." Struggling to hold onto her patience, Hannah grabbed one of the clean shot glasses he had stacked neatly on the back counter and poured a generous amount of the whiskey into it. "I want you to go to my office, pick up the phone, and talk to my aunt. She's on hold."

Deacon narrowed his bright blue eyes and tossed the rag he'd been using on the bar.

"Why?"

Hannah knocked back the shot, sputtered a little, and poured another.

"Because," she said, "I cannot possibly have heard her correctly. I need you to talk to her, and then tell me I'm having either a nightmare or a hallucination."

"What's going on?" he demanded.

"Just go talk to her!" Hannah shouted.

"All right, all right. Jeez." Deacon turned and stalked down the short hallway to Hannah's tiny office.

Hannah chugged the second shot, then picked up his discarded rag and began to polish the top of the old wooden bar. She heard Deacon talking, his voice growing louder, and she polished faster. By the time he slammed back into the taproom, the oak bar gleamed as never before. Hell, she'd practically set the thing on fire.

He walked up to stand beside her, and Hannah stopped her manic polishing to look at him. The expression on his face made her heart fall through the soles of her feet, down into the basement.

Oh, God.

She cleared her throat.

"Aunt Hildy didn't really say that Uncle George emptied my business bank account, took all of my money, and left town with his assistant, did she?"

"Bastard." Deacon said.

Oh, God. It was real.

Hannah's knees gave out, and she sank to the floor behind the bar. It was clean, but she wouldn't have noticed if she'd stuck to the vinyl.

"Is Aunt Hildy okay?" she asked.

"She actually sounded kind of relieved. Except for the whole money thing. She's sorry about that."

Hannah nodded. That was nice.

Deacon got another glass and poured himself some whiskey from the bottle she'd left on the bar. "She said when she got home from work—"

"She's a cashier at the Wal-Mart."

"—there was a note on the kitchen table telling her George and Crystal—"

"The assistant bimbo."

"—were heading somewhere warm."

"Bastard."

Deacon downed his whiskey. He did not sputter.

"The note said he wanted her to tell you he'd taken your money. He didn't want you to find out when the creditors started calling."

"Decent of him." Hannah dropped her face into her hands.

"Did you check your bank account balance?" Deacon asked. "Maybe George is just playing a practical joke or something."

Yeah. Because George was such a light-hearted trickster.

"I got online while I was on the phone with Hildy. It looks like he left me fifty dollars," she said into her hands.

"If you knew that, why the hell did you bother having me talk to her?"

"I didn't believe it." But it was true. It was all true. "Why did I let him talk me into being my accountant?" she moaned. "Why? I know what he's like. It was only a matter of time before he snapped."

"The bigger question," Deacon said, "is how he got access to your business bank account."

"Oh, that's easy," she said, still not looking up. "I gave him signing authority."

"Uh huh." He paused. "Why?" His voice sounded strained.

"After my father died, before you came back to town, I was really busy, and it was hard to keep ahead of the bookkeeping stuff. Uncle George said he did that kind of thing for other clients." She sighed. "And yes, I know I should have started paying the bills again, once you were working here, and I had more time. But I let him keep doing it. It was nice not to have to worry about everything."

Of course, now she had a bigger issue to worry about than finding the time to write out a couple of checks.

Oddly, when she finally looked at Deacon, he seemed relieved.

"Okay," he said. "So he paid bills for other clients. That means he must be bonded."

She hadn't thought there was anything below the basement,

but she could feel her heart bouncing into a dark pit much further down.

She swallowed.

"Um, bonded?"

"A surety bond," Deacon said. "If he was handling your cash, you made sure that he...was..." His voice trailed off when he saw her expression. They stared at each other in silence for a moment.

Deacon squatted beside her, the material of his jeans stretching across his thighs. "Uncle George wasn't bonded?" he asked carefully.

She shook her head.

"I thought you said he handled money for other clients?"

"Well," she shifted on her butt. "Not exactly their money. For the other clients he handled the books, and they wrote the checks. But he said he would handle the money for me. Because I was family. He gave me a good rate."

"Why didn't you make him get bonded?" Deacon shouted.

"He was my uncle!" Hannah shouted back. "I trusted him!"

Then, to her horror, she started to cry. Deep, gulping sobs. Before she could turn away or try to hide, Deacon heaved a sigh, sat on the floor next to her, and pulled her up against his chest.

"Come on, now," he said, stroking his hand down her back.

"I can't believe Uncle George did this to me! The b... b...bastard."

"It'll be okay," Deacon said, as he held her tighter. His arms were strong and they felt good wrapped around her. Without quite realizing what she was doing, Hannah found herself clinging to him, her fingers knotting in the soft fabric of his dark blue Country Time polo shirt. She hoped she wasn't getting snot all over him.

"All of my money is gone," she sobbed.

"I know, Hannah."

She couldn't seem to stop crying. His chest was warm and broad, and he smelled good, and he was holding her, and he'd never done that before, not even when they'd known each other in high school.

Of course, he was her employee now, so it wasn't surprising he never held her. Employees didn't usually go around holding their employers. It was probably weirding him out that she was crying all over him. She tried to get herself back under control.

Sniffling, she pulled away. He let her go, and they looked at each other. Then he shoved to his feet, reached down, and helped her up. She stood, feeling suddenly awkward, and grabbed a tissue from the box behind the bar, blowing her nose as discreetly as possible.

"Sorry," she muttered.

"Better?" Deacon had backed up a little, but he was still watching her with concern.

He wasn't exactly a handsome man, Hannah thought, considering him. He certainly wasn't pretty like his brother, Sam. Yet somehow his face managed to be both hard and sympathetic, framed by receding brown hair kept so brutally short it was little more than stubble. His profile easily could have been stamped on an ancient Roman coin.

"I guess," she said, suddenly aware of the heat and hardness of his body in the confined space.

When she'd known him in high school, before he'd left home at eighteen to join the army, he'd been young and...soft. The years between then and now, the traveling he'd done, the work on oil rigs and in construction, had added layers of solid muscle to his tall frame and some intriguing lines to his face. She'd heard him say he lifted weights regularly because he didn't want to get a gut.

Whatever he was doing, it really worked for him. They'd had a sharp increase in female customers since he'd started working at the Country Time.

He was a drifter who wouldn't stay in town forever, but while he was here he was a definite asset.

Maybe she could get him to go shirtless while he was tending bar to try and attract more women.

A vision of Deacon, shirtless, and maybe dancing and spinning bottles while he made drinks, flitted through her mind.

Yeah. A *definite* asset.

"You have to revoke George's signing authority," he said, pulling her from her admittedly inappropriate thoughts. "You'd better call the bank and do it right away."

"Sure. Because there's so much money left to worry about."

"You want to get him off the account."

"I know that, Deacon." Just because she'd cried all over the man didn't mean he had the right to treat her like she was a complete idiot.

"And you'll have to report this to the police. You have to tell Chief Kline what happened and swear out an arrest warrant, so George can be found and picked up."

"I know that, too," she muttered, wadding up the tissue and throwing it away. "I'm not completely stupid. I know I have to do that." Her stomach jumped. George might be a thief, but he was still her uncle. It made her a little queasy to think about having her uncle arrested.

Deacon could apparently read her mind. "You have to do this, Hannah," he said.

"I know." Then she turned and left him before she broke down and cried all over him again.

Back in her office, Hannah dropped into her chair and logged onto her online banking site to check her balance one more time. What if she'd made a mistake? What if she'd somehow opened the wrong account, and she still had all of her money, and Deacon was right, and that note from George was some kind of sick practical joke? It could happen.

Nope, she thought, looking at the numbers. No joke.

If only she'd made George get bonded. Then she'd have insurance.

Insurance.

She sat up straighter, hope suddenly zinging through her.

The Country Time carried liability insurance, right? Wasn't there a clause in there somewhere about employees stealing? Wasn't George basically an employee? Maybe she would be covered...?

Fingers scrabbling across the desk, she grabbed the phone and called Chet Hinkle, the local insurance agent who'd been handling their policies forever.

"Hey Chet," she greeted him when he answered, trying to sound casual instead of desperate. "I need to ask you about the Country Time's insurance policies."

"You do?" Chet's voice brightened. "Want to schedule a review?"

"No!" She realized she'd snapped the word and took a deep breath before continuing. "No. I, um, was wondering if I was covered for, uh, employee theft."

"Employee theft?" Now Chet sounded confused. "Are you having a problem?"

"Of course not. I'm just interested." She gripped the phone receiver tighter. "Can you look at my policy?"

"Sure. Now?"

"Yes." Hannah tried not to grind her teeth. "Now."

"Sure, okay. Hold on and let me get your file."

After what seemed to be an interminable length of time he was back, huffing slightly, as if moving from his chair had taken an effort.

"Okay," he said and she heard papers flipping in the background. "Let's see what we've...huh."

Hannah's blood chilled.

"What?" she demanded.

"Huh," Chet repeated. "Hmmm...uh huh. Oh."

"For God's sake, what?" He was killing her.

"I remember this now," Chet sounded cheery again, happy things were falling into place. "Before your father died, I met with him, and he cut back on the Country Time's insurance coverage. My note says he wanted to reduce premiums."

"Okay," Hannah said slowly. "And what does that mean for employee theft coverage?"

"Well..." More rustling. "According to the file, he reduced employee theft coverage to a thousand dollars. With the deductible, that's basically nothing." He laughed. "Guess he trusted his employees more than you do, Hannah."

Hope no longer zinged. "I guess," she croaked.

"Hey, it's all there in the addendum," Chet told her. "Didn't you read your insurance policies when you took over the business?"

She hadn't. She'd been too busy coping with her father's death and trying to run the Country Time without quite enough staff. Maybe George would have mentioned it to her if George had been a better adviser. But it was pretty obvious now that he'd been following his own agenda.

Chet must have shifted to the computer while she'd been absorbing the new blow he'd just delivered, because the sound of tapping keys had replaced the shuffling of paper in the background.

"Looks like you still haven't paid your premiums for the quarter," he said, sounding genuinely concerned for the first time in their conversation. "Better tell George to get that check out. You don't want them to lapse."

Right.

"Sure you don't want to review your policies?" Chet sounded hopeful. "I could come over and—"

She hung up on him.

Running her hands through her hair, she tried to think. Apparently insurance would not be riding to her rescue.

Thanks, Dad.

Of course, maybe she should have actually looked at the insurance policies before now.

Her next step was to call the bank to cut off Uncle George's access to the Country Time's checking account. On a whim, she asked the woman who'd answered the phone if they would replace her funds.

Once the woman had stopped laughing, Hannah made an appointment to see a lending officer about reactivating a line of credit her father had taken out a few years ago. She hadn't needed to use it since his death, but she was going to need it now. Big time.

After the bank, she called Police Chief Jacqueline Kline to see what she had to do to have her late mother's older brother arrested. Josie Kline, Chief Kline's daughter and one of Hannah's best friends since sixth grade, had always said her mother was scary protective when it came to people she cared about. So, Hannah wasn't entirely surprised when the other woman said she'd be over in a few minutes to personally take her statement.

Because the Country Time had just opened, Hannah asked the chief to come to the back door in the hopes of avoiding stirring up the customers. As promised, the other woman arrived fifteen minutes later, a young patrolman in tow. As soon as she stepped into the kitchen, she wrapped Hannah in a tight, motherly embrace before letting her go to study her face, her brown eyes serious.

"What the hell happened?"

Hannah shrugged. "I told you on the phone. George ran off with all of the money."

Chief Kline nodded, took off her uniform hat and ran a hand through her cap of dark hair. "I need the details. Tell me everything."

"Okay," Hannah sighed. "We'd better go to the office."

She led them to the office through a side door so they wouldn't have to go into the taproom. But she knew her attempts at discretion had probably been a complete waste of time. Sure enough, when she relieved Deacon at the bar so he could go talk to the chief, she got enough speculative glances to assure her everyone knew something was up.

At least June and Mary Alice, the two servers scheduled for the evening, weren't there yet. Hannah did not look forward to telling June what had happened. The woman wouldn't hesitate to let her know she'd been a complete dumbass.

Then there was Grace, the other server. Kevin, her part-time cook. Jason, the second bartender. Billy, the dishwasher. God, what was she going to tell them? What *could* she tell them?

Maybe she just wouldn't tell them anything.

Hannah considered that option while she drew a beer from one of the taps for a bowling league guy who'd come in early for a pre-game brew. She frowned into the mug as she filled it, ignoring the way the man watched her with ill-disguised curiosity.

No. She had to tell the staff. Hell, at the rate things were going, they'd hear the gossip before they got to work.

Deacon came back behind the bar and touched her shoulder without speaking. Hannah nodded in acknowledgment, gave the bowling league guy his beer, and went back to her office.

Once Chief Kline and her officer were satisfied they'd gotten all of the information they needed for now, Hannah ushered them out through the kitchen. Thank God Kevin hadn't been scheduled to work; it was still deserted.

"We'll do all we can, Hannah," the chief said, after she'd sent her officer out to the car. "I'll put out a warrant on George, so if anyone checks they'll know he's wanted. We'll freeze his accounts, flag his credit cards, and that sort of thing."

"What about Aunt Hildy?" Hannah asked, alarmed.

"I'm going to go talk to her now. We'll see what we can do."

"Thanks." Hannah shook her head. "I just don't understand why the bank didn't call me when the account was emptied."

Chief Kline shrugged. "Why would they? George had signing authority, so he could basically do whatever he wanted. The online records you showed me indicate he transferred the money to a variety of accounts. Your bank probably hasn't even noticed."

"Wonderful." Why the hell was she paying those monthly account fees if the bank wasn't even looking at her account?

Chief Kline cleared her throat. "The problem is, if he closed the other accounts and pulled out the cash, or if he transferred the money from them to other identities, we're going to have a hard time finding him."

"Yeah," Hannah sighed. For all she knew, Uncle George had set up twenty false identities.

"I have a small department," Chief Kline said. "I barely have enough people to handle traffic accidents and the occasional drunk and disorderly. I'll bump this up to the staties, but you're going to need a lawyer, Hannah. And if you want to find George before he spends all of your money, I think you should consider hiring a private investigator."

Hannah stared at the other woman. "And pay him with what? My charm?"

Chief Kline nodded. "Good point." She settled her hat more firmly on her head and patted Hannah's cheek. "I'll be in touch."

"Thank you," Hannah said, meaning it.

"Just doing my job." The chief grinned at her, then tapped her on the nose. "Call Josie. If my girl hears about this from someone else, she's going to be pissed, and I don't want her bitching at me."

Hannah's stomach clutched. "Yes, ma'am."

Chief Kline chuckled and left.

Hannah went back to her office, closed the door, and sat behind her desk, rubbing at the wicked throbbing in her temples. She considered calling Josie and getting it over with, but she just couldn't face her friend.

She checked her bank balance again, instead.

Still fifty dollars.

And she was still screwed.

Handling Love

ALSO BY BETSY HORVATH

WELCOME TO HARDY FALLS

Believing Love

Handling Love

Trusting Love

Expecting Love (novella)

Choosing Love

LOVE'S MOST WANTED

Hold Me

ABOUT THE AUTHOR

Betsy Horvath was raised on a steady diet of old MGM musicals, Nancy Drew, and Harlequin romances, so nobody should have been shocked to discover that one day she would be writing romance novels of her own. Especially not once became clear that, when given the opportunity, she could sing the entire soundtrack from the *Sound of Music*, regardless of whether or not anyone asked her to (nobody ever did), and that the only books she ever wanted to read were the ones with happy endings (which made things interesting in college).

Let's face it, Betsy is a hopeless romantic. But she's good with it.

www.BetsyHorvath.com
betsyhorvath@betsyhorvath.com

9 781943 725045